THE GOLD WATCH

Locked Room
International

Paul Halter books from Locked Room International:
The Lord of Misrule (2010)
The Fourth Door (2011)
The Seven Wonders of Crime (2011)
The Demon of Dartmoor (2012)
The Seventh Hypothesis (2012)
The Tiger's Head (2013)
The Crimson Fog (2013)
The Night of the Wolf (2013)
The Invisible Circle (2014)
The Picture from the Past (2014)
The Phantom Passage (2015)
Death Invites You (2016)
The Vampire Tree (2016)
The Madman's Room (2017)
The Man Who Loved Clouds (2018)

Other impossible crime novels from Locked Room International:
The Riddle of Monte Verita (Jean-Paul Torok) 2012
The Killing Needle (Henry Cauvin) 2014
The Derek Smith Omnibus (Derek Smith) 2014
The House That Kills (Noel Vindry) 2015
The Decagon House Murders (Yukito Ayatsuji) 2015
Hard Cheese (Ulf Durling) 2015
The Moai Island Puzzle (Alice Arisugawa) 2016
The Howling Beast (Noel Vindry) 2016
Death in the Dark (Stacey Bishop) 2017
The Ginza Ghost (Keikichi Osaka) 2017
Death in the House of Rain (Szu-Yen Lin) 2017
The Double Alibi (Noel Vindry) 2018
The 8 Mansion Murders (Takemaru Abiko) 2018
The Seventh Guest (Gaston Boca) 2018

Bibliography
Locked Room Murders Second Edition, Revised 2018

Visit our website at www.mylri.com or
www.lockedroominternational.com

THE GOLD WATCH

Paul Halter

Translated by John Pugmire

The Gold Watch

This book is a work of fiction. The characters, incidents, and dialogue are drawn from the author's imagination and are not to be construed as real. Any resemblance to actual events or persons, living or dead, is entirely coincidental.

Original French title *La Montre en or*.
Copyright © Paul Halter et Eurydice 2019.
THE GOLD WATCH
English translation copyright © by John Pugmire 2019.

Cover design by Joseph Gérard

For information, contact: pugmire1@yahoo.com

FIRST AMERICAN EDITION
Library of Congress Cataloguing-in-Publication Data
Halter, Paul
[*La Montre en or* English]
The Gold Watch / Paul Halter
Translated from the French by John Pugmire

To Fei Wu, who subtly persuaded me to write this story. P.H.

Principal characters

In the contemporary narrative

André Lévêque, *playwright, obsessed with a mysterious film.*
Célia, *his wife, fashion designer.*
Christine Tissier, *spirited sexagenarian, their neighbour.*
Ambroise Moreau, *psychoanalyst, retired doctor of philosophy.*
Carl Jelenski, *astronomer, living in a converted mill.*
Guy, *childhood friend of André.*
Jean-Paul Lamblin *(Jean-Pierre Langlois), Guy's father.*
Janine Lamblin *(Jeanne Langlois), Guy's mother.*
Rita Messmer, *beautiful German, friend of the Lamblins.*
Heinrich Messmer, *her brother.*

In the narrative from the past

Victoria Sanders, *director of a fabric importing company.*
Daren Bellamy, *her brother, lover of night-life.*
Andrew Johnson, *deputy director of the Sanders company.*
Alice Johnson, *his wife, passionate about embroidery.*
Cheryl Chapman, *ex-model, Andrew's secretary.*
Mr. and Mrs. Benson, *handyman and cook at Raven Lodge.*
Inspector Wedekind, *of Scotland Yard.*
Owen Burns, *dandy detective, well-known to the Yard.*
Achilles Stock, *his faithful friend and confidant.*
Jane Miller, *widow, murdered ten years earlier.*

PROLOGUE

London, October 11, 1901

It was raining heavily in the British capital that night. Behind the swirling curtain of rain, Crescent Alley was no longer recognisable. Just a few hours earlier it had looked like a watercolour, freshly-painted and rich in detail, for it was located in a well-to-do part of the city. But now it seemed as though the canvas had been repainted in a much darker colour to represent nightfall, and white traces had been added to evoke the intensity of the rain, whose incessant patter had muffled all other sounds.

The clock of a nearby church could scarcely be heard as it struck ten. The feeble lights of the street lamps fought in vain against the darkness. Just when it seemed there was not a soul around, a figure emerged suddenly from a passageway. It was a woman of some fifty years of age. Clad in a dark cloak, her shoulders hunched and her hat crammed down over her face, she walked briskly, sticking close to the railings of the houses. Then, raising her head, she slowed down before coming to a halt. Her expression of astonishment seemed hardly justified; the house she was looking at appeared no different from its neighbours: a solid brick edifice with lights in two of its windows. Furthermore, she knew it well: it was number 8, her own home. Despite the rain, she stood there perplexed for several moments before a metallic noise at her feet drew her attention. Looking down, she saw a flash of gold, just before the object disappeared behind the railings. The woman let out a deep sigh, cursing the bad luck which, she felt, had followed her all day. And with reason, it must be said, given the events which were soon to follow....

Her precious gold fob watch, which was of great sentimental value to her, had just fallen out of her pocket and bounced to the side into a spot almost impossible to reach. She bent forward awkwardly, slid her hand through the railings, and patted the ground without success. The sought-for object lay beyond her reach, glinting provocatively in

9

the rain. Several long seconds elapsed before she decided to kneel down on the rain-splattered pavement. Long seconds which, it was said afterwards, sealed her fate.

Turning her head to facilitate her outreach, she noticed a furtive figure on the other side of the street. It disappeared into a doorway as soon as she turned to look. Instinctively, she felt there was something menacing about it. Fear gripped her like a vice. Panic seized her as she stood up and hastened in the opposite direction, as if to distance herself from imminent danger. She might have been better advised to spend a few seconds unlocking her own front door and sheltering behind it. But the woman wasn't thinking any more and she ran breathlessly into the passageway from whence she had come. The figure, which had observed her every move from the darkness of a porch, followed her.

At one of the upper windows of number 11, a face pressed against the rain-streaked glass had attentively followed what had happened. It was that of a ten-year-old boy, and what he had just witnessed was strange enough to have held his attention. But from there to alerting his parents… All he would have earned was a good spanking for still being at the window at that time of night.

A few moments later, inside the entrance to the passageway, the breathless woman saw a silhouette on the opposite wall, brilliantly lit by a street lamp. She realised then that her fears were well-founded. Someone had followed her and cleverly manoeuvred himself so as to corner her. Paralysed with fright, her eyes widened and froze. In her dilated pupils he could be seen advancing slowly and relentlessly towards her. She opened her mouth to scream, but no sound came out. A terrifying clap of thunder reverberated in her brain….

1

THE SPIDER'S WEB

June 5, 1991

In her garden, bathed in the morning sunlight, Célia Lévêque looked dreamily at the complex and sophisticated structure stretching between her rosebush and the low wall near the entrance to her property. An appreciative smile crossed her lips. There was something fascinating about this spider's web, still covered with pearls of dew. The cunning design, the strict geometric arrangement, subtly imperfect yet touched by inspiration, made it a work of art. Just like her own creations....

Célia was a fashion designer for a Parisian couturier, where she only went one or two days a week. The rest of the week she worked at home, in the peaceful little village of Orville, near Fontainebleau, where she and her husband had settled a few months ago. Célia was a perfectionist. She didn't limit herself to new designs: when she had the time, she created early samples of her work with needle and thread. Like the spider, which she could now see, hidden in a shady corner of its web.

She smiled to herself. What would André, her husband, have said if she had made a connection between herself and a spider? Comparing that revolting, hairy, many-legged creature to herself, Célia Lamblin, a young and svelte blonde in her thirties, a Grace Kelly look-alike! At least, that's what he'd said whilst he was courting her... Even though love was said to be blind, she knew she was far from repulsive. Her mirror reminded her of the fact as she was trying on her own designs. The regular oval of her face, framed by blonde locks, her sparkling blue eyes and her supple figure... There was definitely something of the famous actress about her!

She was at that point in her thoughts when she noticed her neighbour, Christine Tissier, coming along the street towards her. An amiable sixty-year-old, she was never at a loss for words. With her boyish haircut and her richly-coloured scarf eternally knotted around her neck, she was noticeable from afar. In fact, it was no surprise to see her, for she invariably went shopping at this hour—it was nine-o'clock—when she was in the country; Christine was frequently abroad. Célia was willing to bet that her neighbour would stop by for a chat, and she was soon proved right.

A few moments later, the bubbly and voluble Christine was at her side, lauding the magnificent spider's web which, according to her, was one of the marvels of nature.

'Contrary to what people think,' asserted Christine, in her throaty voice, 'spiders aren't harmful. Apparently they are very beneficial to the planet,' she continued in a scholarly manner. 'They are incredibly numerous and can be found everywhere but at the poles. You mustn't try to kill them.'

'Believe me, I wouldn't dream of it,' replied Célia, laughing. 'And I bet they'll even protect my roses.'

'They're really beautiful,' enthused Christine. 'You're very lucky, Célia. And I'm not just talking about the roses. Maybe you don't realise it at your age, where happiness appears to be the most natural thing in the world. But, as time goes by....'

'Oh, you know, nothing's perfect. There's always something that's not going well....'

'That's so true,' agreed Christine solemnly, observing her neighbour furtively. 'But, just to put my mind at rest... it's nothing serious, I hope?'

'No, I was speaking generally.'

After an awkward silence, Christine continued in a lighter tone:

'And how's your husband? We don't see much of him in the village.'

'Oh, he's always locked away in his office, lost in thought. You know how artists are... When they're in a creative phase, they ignore the world around them. Contrary to you and me, for example, André would walk right past this spider's web without seeing it. Unless he'd decided to use it in one of his intrigues....'

'I understand.'

Christine knew, needless to say, that André Lévêque was a playwright. She'd had long conversations with Célia on the subject. He'd had a huge success with his first work, *The Son of Pasiphaë*, which she had liked very much. His next work, *The Man of Wax*, had had a favourable reception, but nothing more. He knew that, unless his next play was a success, he would soon be forgotten. He'd been working hard for several weeks now, but so far in vain.

'I must admit that he's not at his best, these days,' sighed Célia.

'Ah?' exclaimed Christine, affecting an air of surprise and trying hard not to show her curiosity.

'Creativity isn't something you can just order.'

'Of course.'

'Even so, I think there's something else. He's fixated on a distant memory. It's something fairly trivial, but it seems to be causing writer's block. It's going to become insurmountable if he can't solve it soon. I keep telling him that the more he thinks about it, the less likely he is to remember. But what I say doesn't have any effect. It's becoming an obsession.'

'A troubling memory? Is it something personal or intimate?'

'Oh, no. At least, not in the sense you mean. It's more like a childish whim.'

'I see... more or less. But you needn't tell me if. ...'

Célia laughed disarmingly:

'It's not really a mystery. It's ridiculous to attach such importance to something so trivial. I've told him so repeatedly, and he agrees, but he simply must know, must find this film, whose name he doesn't even know, but whose images marked his childhood and, he says, was the inspiration for his playwriting career.'

'Find the name of a film?' echoed Christine in astonishment. 'Is that all?'

'Yes, a film, which he didn't even see in its entirety, just a few images from a trailer! I know, making such a fuss about it is incomprehensible to most people... He's done a lot of research, skimmed through a lot of old films, consulted cinema enthusiasts... but without success so far.'

There was a silence, punctuated by the merry chirping of sparrows. Christine Tissier, her eyes riveted on the spider's web, thought furiously and then announced:

'I think I know someone who could help.'

'Here in the village?'

'Yes, in fact I can think of two people. Do you know Carl Jelenski?'

'The name rings a bell. Isn't he that foreigner who lives in a converted mill?'

'That's right. People don't know him because he rarely leaves his lair. He looks like an old owl, but he's a remarkable astronomer.'

'Really? And how could he help André?'

'He sees things that others miss. At least, that's what he claims. I took him for a bit of a crank, but he's surprised me a couple of times by his strangely prophetic remarks. Anyway, it wouldn't cost you anything to see him. He's always pleased to have a little company. But, most of all, I was thinking of Dr. Ambroise Moreau.'

'The balding old gentleman who lives near the forest?'

'He's only sixty,' said Christine charitably.

'Of course… I didn't know he was a doctor.'

'He's a doctor of philosophy, but he occasionally practices psychoanalysis.'

'Psychoanalysis? But André doesn't need….'

'He's also a very knowledgeable cinema enthusiast, particularly about old films. Add to that his intelligence and his familiarity with psychology… And, besides, he's a very charming man. He would also be pleased to listen to your husband. He could be of great help.'

'Well,' said Célia, seemingly embarrassed, 'thank you very much! I'll talk to André. I'm sure he'll be interested. It's a spot of luck that you happened to pass by.'

'Oh, it's nothing,' replied Christine, pointing to the spider. 'That's whom you have to thank. Spinning the threads of fate….'

'Well, I promise to leave it in peace!'

'Regarding that film,' said Christine thoughtfully, adjusting her scarf. 'You spoke about images affecting your husband.'

'Yes, indeed.'

'Do you remember what they were about, exactly?'

'Of course!' replied Célia, shrugging her shoulders. 'We've talked about it enough! Very banal things. At least, banal for a detective film. A sinister passageway, heavy rain, black railings, and a terrified woman….'

2

THE GOLD WATCH

June 10, 1991

Ambroise Moreau's vast drawing room was bathed in a soft half-light, which came from a single table lamp, discreetly placed at the far end of the room. Its rays illuminated the gold bindings of the numerous books on the shelves, and sculpted the features of the master of the house in copper tones. He was an imposing, well-built man with thinning hair, combed back, and large, hirsute hands. Occasionally, the look in his small blue eyes would harden, but only when he was concentrating, at which time he would chew on the frame of the glasses he wore for reading. Firmly ensconced in his armchair, he dominated his visitor, who was seated in one corner of a couch staring into space. Somewhere between thirty and forty years old, of medium height, and with short black hair, André Lévêque possessed no distinctive features, except perhaps for his sad, dreamy expression. But, for now, that expression was indecipherable.

'I prefer to influence you as little as possible, André—if you will permit me to call you that,' declared Dr. Moreau. 'First, I'd like you to go over the facts in chronological order, stressing what's most important to you. That will enable me to get the general idea. Only then should we go over things in greater detail. I hope the lighting of the room doesn't strike you as too theatrical, but I've learned from experience that it helps concentration and sharpens the senses. It's important that you feel completely at ease. And I fully understand that, for personal reasons, you prefer that some of the persons and places remain anonymous. That won't be a problem, I assure you.'

André Lévêque swallowed hard several times before beginning:

'I must have been about ten years old, more or less. I can't be more accurate, unfortunately. Guy was my childhood friend—my best friend at the time. He was very clever and full of ideas, and it was at his house where I saw the film... or, rather, the trailer. Images which

have left their mark on me forever. In those days—the mid-sixties—
we didn't have a television set. It was a luxury item. Guy was the only
one of my friends to have one, and it was the first time I'd ever seen a
detective film. Whenever I'd been to a cinema with my parents, it was
always to see a cartoon like *Snow White* or *Peter Pan*. In those days,
it was unthinkable to show tales of murder to children! I must have
seen the trailer two or three times, on the days when the complete
film was due to be shown. I was so full of morbid curiosity that I
pestered my mother to be allowed to see it at my friend's house. I can
still hear her reply: "It's completely out of the question. Those Fritz
Lang horror stories are not for someone your age." In fact, she was
wrong, it wasn't a Fritz Lang film—and that mistake put me off the
scent for a long time. Despite her admonishment, I was determined to
see it secretly with my friend, but unfortunately his television set had
broken down. Anyway, those details are unimportant. Getting back to
the images themselves, there was first a shot of the house in the rain,
with its sinister atmosphere, then a disturbing roving figure... Then a
close-up of the pavement, with the rain streaming on it and the
railings in the background... There was a strange, macabre detail on
the ground... Something shiny, no doubt a precious object... A door-
knob turning slowly... Then another close-up of a terrified old
woman... as if she were about to be murdered.

'At the beginning, I was just frustrated not to have my curiosity
satisfied. The years went by and I developed a taste for mystery
stories by reading lots of Agatha Christie books and several films,
such as *Psycho* and *23 Steps to Baker Street*, the only two to make me
shiver as much as that mysterious trailer. I told myself that I was
bound to see it on television eventually, and that turned out to be the
case. But I had other interests at the time—I must have been about
twenty—such as drinking, playing the guitar and chasing girls. I did
see the trailer and promised myself to see the whole film. But on the
night it was broadcast I was very sleepy—no doubt after a heavy
night-before—and fell asleep halfway through. All I remember is that
the story was less terrifying than I had imagined, more detective than
macabre, and the identity of the murderer was pretty obvious. I
couldn't tell you any more about the story, but I do remember the
sequence of the door-knob turning, which seemed to occur in two
stages. The knob turned as the murderer tried to get into the house,

but in vain. The door was bolted. There was a close-up of a woman's frightened face as she had her back against the door, and the scene was repeated a second time. In fact, the only new element in that second occurrence in the film was the presence of a large white spiral staircase in the house. The final scene took place upstairs. That's just about all I can remember with certainty... except that the director wasn't Fritz Lang. Nor was it Hitchcock, because I would have remembered that. As for the title, it was nothing striking. I promised myself I'd make a note of it later, but I overestimated my memory and it's vanished forever.

'The years went by and I started to write mystery plays... As my success built, I thought more and more about that film and those images. I asked around: friends versed in the subject, detective story lovers and film buffs, but nothing. Nobody could name the mysterious film. I followed countless false trails in vain.

'Recently, I decided to tackle the problem head-on. I owe it to myself. I don't know how to explain it, but I sense that it's vital for my career and my equilibrium. It's a bit like salmon swimming upstream to find their birthplace. That film gave birth to me, in a sense. And I have to know who my father is, do you understand?'

'Perfectly,' declared Dr. Moreau in his soothing voice, which contrasted with André's disjointed, hesitant delivery. 'The fruits of your imagination are at risk, and we mustn't lose the roots of the tree. I sincerely believe I can help you, even though I don't know precisely how at this moment, despite being very familiar with the films of the sixties. Not so much those involving mysteries, although I do have friends who can help there.

'I have to say that the details you've supplied are rather meagre. Or, if you prefer, typical of the genre. A sinister figure, a house in the rain, a frightened woman, a slowly-turning door-knob, a staircase... basic fare in almost every film of suspense. There must be a hundred titles corresponding to that description. What I suggest you do first is to draw up a precise list of all the elements, noting the degree of certitude for each. Once you've done that, we can start our search.'

After a pause, the psychoanalyst added:

'But I caution you to be very careful, and as impartial as possible, because the memory is dangerously subjective. Particularly in individuals like yourself, blessed with great sensitivity.'

'Is it as obvious as that?' asked André, with a pout which was at once sad and amused.

'Doesn't your profession require you to immerse yourself for long hours in imaginary worlds cut off from daily life? Your memory is inevitably influenced by the romantic and the nostalgic. In your case, the blessed days of your childhood, a fabulous period of discovery, including violent sentiments, such as fear... We like fear just as much as happiness: children adore stories about ogres and witches. Now, you need to realise that nostalgia is a more powerful force than love. If you will, it's like a lost happiness we know we'll never be able to find again. An impossible love might eventually blossom, but an event in the past will stay there forever. So, perfidious nostalgia must be avoided like the plague. The danger is that it will forge details more wished-for than real....'

'And thus alter my memories?'

'Exactly. Memory is already complex enough without interference from agents of distortion.'

With a smile of barely-suppressed vanity, Dr. Moreau added:

'That said, it's a subject I've pretty well mastered. We're going to be crafty and turn our enemy's weapons against him.'

'I'm afraid I don't follow you.'

'We're going to use nostalgia, or more precisely, feebleness of sentiment, to our advantage.'

André shook his head desolately:

'I still don't understand...'

The psychoanalyst raised his hand, as if to appeal for calm, then asked:

'What is memory, for you? Or, what does it make you think of, in imagery?'

'Er... a mass of grey matter.'

'We're used to more imagination from you than that, M. Lévêque, if you'll permit me to say so. Think of something utterly banal which we see everywhere, in attics, in gardens... I won't keep you in suspense. Personally, I know no better example than a spider's web.'

'A spider's web?' repeated André in surprise. 'That's funny, my wife was talking about that recently. There's a beautiful example of that in our garden, which...'

'It's what it represents that interests us. Imagine that the elusive

18

memory is the spider's prey, and it's trapped in a network of threads. The more numerous they are, the more tightly it's held. The more numerous the links to a particular memory are, the more it's anchored in the brain.'

André nodded his head:

'Yes, I understand.'

'Those links are sometimes tenuous, and need to be reinforced as much as possible, recognising that emotional ones are the most powerful. You might forget the name of an acquaintance, but never that of a son. Or, let's take the example of the cinema. Some people can recite the names of hundreds of actors and directors without difficulty. Are they blessed with a prodigious memory? Not at all. They just know all the gossip and anecdotes relative to their favourites: the mistress of one, the enemy of another, the rivalries, the passions; in short, all the human and colourful links which connect that small world. The simple evocation of an actor's name brings up a dozen links instantly. There's nothing magical about it. I know that, in your case, the images are isolated, but together we can re-create a favourable climate... The links will progressively reinforce each other, develop, and re-create, like the monstrous heads of the Hydra.'

'And the memories will flood back as if by magic!'

'Exactly,' agreed Dr. Moreau.

'I agree it's all convincing in theory. But does it work in practice?'

'Trust me, André. Trust my experience and abandon that harmful scepticism. Face the problem calmly. You won't feel any pressure. Let's just say you're simply here to learn, to discover, slowly, without haste, step by step... But, before we go any further, I'd like to share my own point of view with you. I've understood your problem, as you presented it. This unknown film represents a personal challenge for you, almost a professional one. But I fear, based on the manner in which you've recalled it—and, here again, it's my long experience which is talking—that there's something more profound behind it... There are moments when your personality seems to change, as if—.'

The young playwright stiffened.

'Really... I don't see....'

'These images, so vivid, so troubling, may be connected to other memories, more painful, which you're subconsciously rejecting....'

André shook his head with a tense smile:

'No, that would surprise me greatly. I think I would have noticed if that were the case!'

'Very well, let's just leave that to one side, for the time being. In any case, I think we've said enough for today. Let's not force things.' Then, frowning, he added:

'But before you leave, I'd like to go back to one specific point... or "image," let's say. I sensed that... never mind. Relax, close your eyes, and try to project yourself back to the time when you were ten years old... Think about your friend Guy, his house, and the room with the television set... Can you still see it?'

'Yes, more or less. The television stand was near a pair of long windows opening on to the garden, with a large plant to one side.'

'Do you remember what the weather was like, when you saw the trailer?'

'Well, yes, I saw it twice. Once, in the late afternoon, the weather was lousy.'

'Lousy, as in the film... It was raining... Maybe you could hear it pattering on the pavement... Something fell on to that wet pavement, something shiny, like a precious object...Try to see that scene again... I don't think it was a long object, such as a knife or a pistol, otherwise you would have probably remembered.'

'Yes, you're right,' murmured André, his eyes closed. 'It was something more compact...'

'Maybe a round object?'

'Yes, possibly.'

'A jewel? A ring?'

'No, that seems too small... But it was round and big enough to see.'

'A fob watch? A gold watch?'

André frowned for a minute, then suddenly opened his eyes wide:

'A gold watch,' he stammered. 'Yes, that's it. *It was a gold watch*!'

3

"EVE IN THE ORIENT"

January 7, 1911

Sitting upright in a corner of the couch, apparently embroidering a place mat, Alice Johnson observed her husband out of the corner of her eye. Standing near the mantelpiece, he was fiddling with his fob watch, as he did automatically when there was something on his mind. A gold fob watch with a chain of the same metal across the waistcoat: the symbol of a successful businessman, which Andrew had undoubtedly become. As if that were necessary, his grey three-piece suit added to the impression, and even aged him a little. Setting aside his stuffy appearance, he was a broodingly handsome man in his thirties. But how he had changed since joining the London-based Sanders company, where he had rapidly climbed to the top. Alice had met him many years earlier, when he was living a Bohemian life and passionately interested in painting and the theatre. Whilst seemingly inclined to become an actor, he had painted a canvas which had changed his life completely, as if Fate had intervened to point him in the opposite direction. Today, he was nothing less than the right hand of the owner of the company, Victoria Sanders, who also happened to be their hostess for a few days, here at Raven Lodge, an imposing country house at the edge of the woods surrounding the tiny village of Broomfield. Had she really thought it would be a good idea to invite a small group of guests for a long weekend in this glacial beginning of January? Even though some of the guests were yet to arrive, the tension was already palpable... Only the future would tell, thought Alice, biting her lip. Everything would already have been decided if the weekend had fallen during the festive season, as originally planned. But unresolved company issues had forced its delay, and between times a heavy fall of snow had occurred, so that Raven Lodge, now encircled by virgin snow, appeared even more isolated. It was not the first time Alice had visited Victoria's second home, and it had always given her a strange feeling. This time it was even worse, like an icy apprehension which she knew was not entirely due to the outside temperature.

'What are you thinking about, darling?' Andrew asked her point-blank, after consulting his watch, which was showing five o'clock.

'About that stuck-up tart Cheryl, who still hasn't arrived... What an idea to invite her. Not to mention that ill-bred lout Daren.'

'He's just left for London and won't be back until tomorrow.'

'I know, and I'm glad. His presence makes me uneasy, the way he looks at me. We need to talk about it seriously, Andrew.'

After running his hands nervously through his hair, her husband replied:

'All right. But later. I need to see the boss about business. She wants to see me, and you know how strict she is about punctuality.'

'About business... ah, well,' she sighed. 'There was I thinking we were on holiday.'

Her husband hardly paid attention. He was already striding towards the door.

A few moments later, he was in Victoria Sanders' office.

The room was similar to her London office. The walls were covered with richly-coloured drapes, which lent warmth to the rather functional furniture. The mistress of the house, who was sitting on her chair with a thoughtful finger on her lips, seemed quite small in front of her imposing mahogany desk. She was about the same age as Andrew, and it was difficult to envisage her as the director of the house of Sanders, a post previously held by her late husband, who was much older, and who had engaged her as a simple secretary before asking for her hand. A marriage of love? Of business? A mixture of the two? Only the two of them knew. Small, as thin as a rake, with an emaciated face and an aquiline nose, a yellowish complexion, and straight black hair, Victoria was anything but pretty. Her strengths lay elsewhere: incisive, determined, straightforward, courageous and highly competent. If he could have seen her, her husband would not have regretted leaving her his company, which she directed with an iron hand and great efficiency. But the portrait would not be complete without mentioning her sensitivity to art and other beautiful things, which were, incidentally, part of her work, as we shall see.

22

'Take a seat, Andrew,' she said without preamble, indicating a chair facing her. 'I'm sorry to be talking business during these rare moments of relaxation, but the news is not good... Do you remember Kalyan?'

'Of course, madam. Kalyan Hiresh of Jaipur, our best pattern designer. Our Chhipa dyers swear by him. He's been responsible for our best fabrics, the most sought-after ones—.'

'Well, he's dead,' cut in Victoria. 'I've just received a letter to that effect.'

Andrew grimaced. 'That's quite a blow. I know no one's irreplaceable, but in his case....'

'He was also a friend. I only met him a few times, but we hit it off right away... And he always refused the salary increases I proposed, saying that between us friends, there could be no question of money.'

She fell silent for a moment, swallowing hard. A distant look came into her eyes:

'Death is a strange thing, whose concept varies considerably between different peoples. A sad event for some, a cause for celebration for others, the beginning of a new life for many Hindus...'

'Are you talking about reincarnation?'

Victoria gave a rueful smile:

'It would certainly be helpful if Kalyan returned to us! But I fear it would be in another form, maybe animal, but in any case without his savoir-faire... Frankly, I don't know anything at the moment, and I haven't really thought about it as far as it concerns me.'

Andrew was about to repeat that his death was the least desirable thing in the world, but he bit his tongue. Victoria hated anything maudlin.

'Do you remember the first time we met, Andrew?' she asked in a different tone of voice.

'Of course! How could I not? You've transformed my life, as if by a magic wand.'

With a gentle smile, Victoria replied:

'On the contrary, it is you, Andrew, who has brought me a great deal. The Sanders company owes much of its success to your sense of colour, and to your know-how, as an artist as well as a businessman. I understood that the moment I set eyes on your painting. I knew you

23

were a man of sound taste, a future and precious collaborator in the choice of our fabrics. Your work spoke for you: that audacious mix of turquoise, orange and violet, sublimating feminine grace, in the form of a ravishing Eve...'

How could Andrew ever forget that moment? In the depths of despair from lack of public interest, and having decided that his current exhibition of paintings would be his last, there was someone practically swooning over his "Eve in the Orient," which he considered one of his minor works—too classic, but for the audacious colours. She had proposed an extravagant sum, and—taking his dumbfounded silence as a challenge—had promptly doubled it. Moreover, on the following day, when she dropped by to collect her purchase, she had made him a very attractive offer of employment. And, in only a few years, he had become deputy director.

'Yes,' Victoria continued, 'it was a lucky day for me when I met you, and I've never regretted it... But I wanted to talk to you about something else... You see, I'm beginning to wonder whether our partnership was a good idea.'

'Oh?' replied Andrew in astonishment. 'Why, may I ask? Business has never been better.'

'Please don't try to smooth things over. I'm not blind, as you know perfectly well. My brother Daren is a detestable human being, a good-for-nothing and a parasite, who only comes to see me when he needs money. I've given in to his whining far too often, but on his last visit I told him that was it, and from then on he had to act like an adult and earn his living, just like everyone else. I thought he'd learnt his lesson, because he hadn't shown his face here for some time. But I was wrong. He hasn't changed in the least. He's still as arrogant, provocative and dissolute as ever... He left for London on the pretext of an urgent business matter, but I'm willing to bet it's to paint the town red, because here he's constrained to a modicum of good behaviour. Well, I can't stop his chasing after anything in skirts... That cannot have escaped your notice! If not, ask your wife. He's been at the limit of crudeness several times.'

The mistress of the house paused and became sober and reflective before continuing:

'But I want to make one thing perfectly clear. Daren is my brother. Even though we couldn't be less alike, we're of the same blood, and linked by a painful past. Whatever mischief he gets up to, no matter how rude he is, I cannot disown him, or take sides against him. Do you understand, Andrew?'

Andrew lowered his eyes:

'Yes, madam, I understand perfectly. I'll make sure there are no problems.'

'Come to think of it, you'll almost certainly be spared the embarrassment tomorrow. You, and above all your wife. He'll probably chase after Cheryl as soon as she sets foot here. Even though she's not the kind of girl I appreciate, I like her personally. You did well to choose her as your secretary. She's serious about her job and really tries her best. I've always believed that willpower beats knowledge. I trust her. I even thought about drawing up a new... Anyway, I'm very indebted to her.'

'Ah? In what way, exactly?'

'In a certain way, she opened my eyes to you.'

Andrew, now on the defensive, frowned and stammered:

'I'm afraid I don't understand...'

Victoria gave him a mischievous smile:

'As soon as I met her for her job interview, I immediately realised the source of your inspiration for that troubling "Eve in the Orient"....'

After leaving and closing the door discreetly behind him, Andrew broke out in a sweat. He knew how to interpret Victoria's last remark. Taking a deep breath, he took a deep breath and walked resolutely to the drawing room where Alice was waiting for him, "wanting to talk," which signified further complications. He found her exactly as he had left her, sitting upright in a corner of the couch, embroidering a place mat. For a few seconds, he forgot his own problems and stared at her as he done on their first meeting. He had always admired her proud bearing, her finely-sculpted features, and her blonde tresses wound in a chignon. All she lacked to resemble the Nordic goddess of love, Freyja, was a fur tunic and a helmet. But she had never sought to be immortalised on canvas. In that way, she was very different from Cheryl... Cheryl, blonde like her, but slightly smaller and with higher cheek bones, more supple and more lascivious in her poses... less rigid, both in reality and figuratively. Alice's clear, precise tones brought him back to the present:

'Is everything all right, darling?'

'Yes, of course. More or less. We've lost our best craftsman... Kalyan, an old Indian gentleman. But I don't suppose his name means much to you.'

'No, it doesn't. But I think I shall lose my patience if things continue as they are.'

'What are you talking about, darling?'

'About Daren, or have you forgotten? I'm not prepared to tolerate his crudeness, his insinuations, or the way he leers at me as if I'm wearing nothing on my back... If that continues, I warn you I'm packing my bags on the spot.'

'Calm down, darling, he's not here right now.'

'And I'm taking advantage of that to raise the subject. And if you're not capable of taking matters in hand, talk to his sister. She'll be able to sort him out, I'm sure.'

Andrew sighed and shook his head:

'He's her brother, Alice, let's not forget that. And don't forget that she's the hand that feeds us, either.'

'Very well, let's talk about Cheryl, your dear secretary....'

Her husband rolled his eyes indignantly:

'Cheryl? What's she got to do with it?'

Tight-lipped, she looked him up and down:

'You disappoint me, Andrew. I thought you were a better actor than that. To start with, can you tell me whose idea it was to invite that little tart here?'

'Victoria's, of course. And if you doubt me, you can ask her yourself. She's still in her office, if it's that important to you.'

'In her office? Perfect. In that case we can take a quick look in her bedroom. I'd like to show you something... I was in there not long ago, entirely by accident, having mistaken the door... and I discovered something I should have realised a long time ago.'

'What? Rummage around in her room? I refuse. It's absolutely not done.'

Alice folded her arms haughtily:

'It's either that, or a scene at dinner. Your choice.'

A few moments later, the two of them were on the landing at the top of the imposing white staircase. Alice went to the door of Victoria's room and stopped to study the chiselled frame.

'These Greek motifs are quite interesting. They're on every door frame. They're classical and modern at the same time.'

'Please, darling. Let me remind you we could be surprised at any moment. Chandra, her faithful Indian manservant, roams the house like a watchdog.'

'Chandra, a watchdog? Strange, I never thought of him like that.'

'Please, let's not lose any more time!'

Once they were inside the room, Alice pointed out a canvas above a chest of drawers, framed by turquoise silk curtains.

'There, darling. You recognise your masterpiece, I assume? What's it called, now? "Sheherazade in Paradise"? "Oriental Dream"?'

'"Eve in Orient,"' he said, wiping his brow.

'That's it. But that's not the question, my dear. It's the subject matter which interests us, the highly provocative young woman who's twisting herself around the trees, clothed in her birthday suit. And, most of all, her face... Does she remind you of anyone?'

'Well....'

'As the painter, you should remember, shouldn't you? Personally, I think there's a curious resemblance to that arrogant minx of a secretary... I can't hear you any more, my dear. Yours is what's called a guilty silence. Why have you never told me that you've known your new secretary for a long time? And that she posed for you as naked as the day she was born?'

'Because,' said Andrew, capitulating, 'because I thought it wasn't necessary for you to know... fearing that you would reproach me exactly as you're doing now. That's it. That's the whole story. And let me remind you that it was this canvas——.'

'I know, this magic canvas changed our lives. Praise be to the marvellous Miss Cheryl! I'm going to thank her personally when she arrives.'

'No you won't, Alice. You're too well brought up for that.'

A long silence reigned as daylight started to fade. Regaining control of herself, Alice sighed:

'Even so, you could have told me, couldn't you?'

Her husband, who seemed not to have heard her, had gone over to the table beside the bed, on which were a bedside lamp and a book with a yellow cover.

'That's odd,' he said.

'What, the book?'

'Yes, I hardly imagined that Victoria would be interested in this kind of reading.'

Alice came to join him and picked it up:

'*The King in Yellow*. That's a strange title.' She flipped through the pages. 'It's only a play. I thought it would be more interesting.' She turned suddenly. 'Footsteps in the corridor, I think.'

After waiting for a few moments, Andrew went to the door, which he opened cautiously. After checking the corridor, he made a sign to his wife:

'There's no one there. Let's go!'

4

THE SPIRAL STAIRCASE

June 11, 1991

The sunlight flooded into Célia's workshop. She stretched voluptuously as she looked around her luminous universe. It was nine o'clock in the morning. She loved nothing more than these moments of calm, where everything seemed to be favourable and her forces were gathered to tackle the day's work in the best possible conditions. It was almost as if the two mannequins on either side of the large pivoting mirror were about to salute her and the brushes and crayons were itching to get going. Then she thought about André, who was still sleeping with clenched fists when she got up. She hadn't spoken to him since his visit to the psychoanalyst. She'd found him in the same state when she'd got back late the night before and hadn't dared to waken him.

With a smile full of tenderness, she went over to the lacquered oriental cabinet where she kept her most precious things. She opened one of the drawers and pulled out an old mauve notebook. Her expression hardened and she closed it immediately. In her haste, she had made a mistake. In the adjacent drawer, she found what she was looking for: a small box. She opened it and placed the contents gently on a table: two pieces from what appeared to be the same seashell. She pieced them together, to verify, for the umpteenth time, their perfect fit... In a film, the same scene would have been accompanied by swelling music. She herself still had trouble believing it... they aligned perfectly, even though a few minuscule fragments had disappeared during the breakage.

It was an extraordinary story, which nobody other than the two of them truly believed... "It's incredible!" André had stammered when he first recognised the phenomenon. "Our story is written in the stars..." Célia had solemnly agreed, prior to them exchanging a long, passionate kiss. It hadn't been the first time they'd met, but it had

29

been the first time they'd been sure they were made for each other.

She had told him about a piece of seashell, given to her by a great-aunt who had told her that its companion was in the possession of a boy she'd met aboard a steamship when she was only a young girl. On the bridge, one marvellous starlit night, he had broken a very pretty shell in two to seal their passion…A fleeting passion, alas, for they had never seen each other again after the voyage. It had been the old lady's most precious possession, and she had given it to Célia with such fervour she had vowed never to be parted from it. André's eyes had widened in surprise when she told him the story, for one of his great-uncles had told him a similar tale. He hadn't remembered any details other than the name of the boat: the Lusitania. But at his death, a small box containing a piece of shell was found, which had ended up in André's possession. A few days later, he and Célia had met again, each secretly praying that the impossible would happen….

André couldn't have chosen a better moment to turn up. Célia threw herself into his arms.

'Ah!' he said, noticing the piece of seashell. 'You need to look at it more frequently, darling.'

'Enough of that! Tell me about last night. How did it turn out? What's the mysterious Dr. Moreau like? Does he live alone?'

'I couldn't say for certain, but there were no signs of a female presence. He was courteous and seemed competent enough.'

And he proceeded to describe his encounter in some detail.

Célia gave a tight-lipped smile and observed:

'A watch… It's not much on its own, but as long as you think it's important….'

'Yes, darling,' replied André fervently. 'For the first time I feel sure I'm on the right track. I'm hopeful it will help me identify the film, and you know how important that is to me.'

'Only too well,' she retorted, looking up at the ceiling. 'And I suppose you'll be seeing him again soon?'

'Yes, at the beginning of next week. The time for him to do some research.'

'Well, you seem to have intrigued him with your story!'

André picked up the piece of shell and held it up to the sun's rays—bringing out tints of iris—before replying, in a solemn voice:

'Yes, but maybe not in the way I'd intended. According to him, there's something more profound behind it. Some troubling memories which he intends to retrieve from my subconscious. What do you think?'

Giving him a lingering look, Célia came into her husband's arms once more.

'I think it's an excellent idea, darling. You excel at bringing out passion in people, and I was your first victim!'

June 17, 1991

His eyes riveted on the porcelain elephant, which shone feebly in the psychoanalyst's dimly-lit drawing room, the young playwright listened attentively to his host.

'We need to be extremely careful, André. This "gold watch" is very important, but I'm worried that I may have forced your hand. I was simply trying to give you a small demonstration.'

'Nevertheless, I'm certain that object—.'

'We'll get back to it. But before that, I'd like to recap the elements at our disposal. According to you, there were two broadcasts. The first one, you guessed, was between 1965 and 1967, and the second between 1978 and 1980. Oddly enough, it's the earlier one which seems the most promising. Why? Because, at that time only Channel 2 was broadcasting American mysteries, and then only sporadically. Compiling a complete list of them should limit our search to a hundred or so films at the most. Take away all of Fritz Lang's work and Hitchcock's, which you've already watched in vain, and all the great classics of the genre, like *The Maltese Falcon* and the unforgettable *Laura*, which you've also screened, and we're down to a maximum of thirty, most of them fairly minor. Following that thinking, the simplest would be to consult the archives of our regional newspaper and note the films from the years 65 to 67... If you're ready to dedicate two or three days of your time....'

'I am,' replied André, almost tearfully. 'How everything seems so simple with you, doctor.'

'Even so, it's far from finished. The titles and summaries of the films could have errors, and, above all, some copies might be almost impossible to find. So, I've taken the initiative of consulting a few friends....'

'And?' asked André anxiously.

'They've turned up three titles,' replied Dr. Moreau, with a mysterious smile, putting on his glasses to consult a piece of paper:

'*Sorry, Wrong Number*, 1948, with Barbara Stanwyck and Burt Lancaster; *The Spiral Staircase*, 1945, with Dorothy McGuire and George Brent; and *The Unseen*, also in 1945, with Gail Russell and Joel McCrea. Do any of them ring a bell?'

'No... wait... the first one sounds vaguely familiar.'

'I remember seeing it myself, but it was a very long time ago and I only remember it vaguely. My friend is going to send me a copy, as well as *The Spiral Staircase,* which sounds the most promising of the three, according to the description. As for *The Unseen,* that's going to be much more difficult, because it's very hard to find, but it's also the least likely of the three. It's about a teacher to whom a widower entrusts his children.'

'That doesn't ring any bells.'

'Let's start with the first two. We'll probably have learnt a few more things whilst we're waiting... But let's get back to our "gold watch," which I'm fearful of having planted in your mind. It's a highly symbolic object, as you probably know. First, there's the gold, which provokes greed. Then there's the watch, with its hands, tangible witnesses to time and life itself passing.'

'I've thought about it a lot since we talked about it,' said André, wiping his brow with the back of his hand. 'You may be right. I do get the feeling that object is related to a distant personal memory--or at least something tied to the time I used to visit my friend Guy... And not just that scene in the film.'

'So talk to me about your friend. What did you like to do together? What games did you play?'

The porcelain elephant faded from André's view, to be replaced by a gently sloping lawn behind his friend's beautiful house. A few flagstones led to the entrance to a garage, which in turn led to a cellar with a ping-pong table. He had spent so many hours of fun there....

'... and, in the room next door there were piles of comic books. Mandrake the Magician, Blake and Mortimer's *The Secret of the Great Pyramid.* I think it was the first time I learnt about the mysteries of ancient Egypt... And all those test tubes. We did chemistry experiments, which got us into trouble with his parents when the sulphurous smells reached the parlour floor... Also, I remember we worked really hard to make a boomerang. Meticulous cuts of the saw, careful sanding, delicate rounding of the ends, followed by several coats of varnish. Once again, we were sharply reprimanded by his father, Jean-Paul Lamblin, a very strict man. Or, at least, that's how he appeared to me at the time. We were immediately to stop making something which could be dangerous. It's true that we'd done a number of things which had made him—and particularly his wife Janine, a worrier by nature—anxious. The truth is, they were both very nice to me. One evening, they'd taken me to a pizzeria for the first time in my life. My parents couldn't afford to do so. I was overjoyed, but M. Lamblin spoilt it for me by reprimanding me for holding my fork the wrong way. On the other hand....'

'Yes?' prompted Dr. Moreau, when his guest failed to continue.

'There's something strange... His behaviour was sometimes paradoxical. I don't know why I'm saying that, but it will come to me another time. Then came that famous autumn, when I saw the trailer.'

'Autumn? That's new, and it could help refine our search. Are you sure?'

'Yes, I believe so. The days had become overcast and rainy.'

And, for the umpteenth time, André related the circumstances in which he had discovered the troubling trailer. But this time there were more details, thanks to the artful prompting of the psychoanalyst. The environment and the actors were becoming clearer.

'There were, of course, M. and Mme. Lamblin. No, wait a minute. Mme. Lamblin was no longer there. She'd already had her tragic accident the year before... There were friends. A beautiful German girl, I remember, and her brother who had a very Germanic name, Heinrich. A very discreet individual, almost insignificant. They used to visit from time to time. What was her name?... Rita, I think. I recall them quite clearly because of their nationality. The last war was on their minds a lot, and the wounds were hard to heal. Having German friends was not the done thing at the time. Rita had beautiful black, shining hair, which contrasted with her red lips. She had a ravishing smile and always wore dark tailored dresses in black or violet. A sort of Snow White, but older... I don't know why I'm telling you all this.'

33

Dr. Moreau nodded his head thoughtfully, stroking his chin. In a low voice, he declared:

'It may be more important than you think. To the point that I'm debating whether we should continue these sessions.'

'Why?' replied André anxiously. 'Aren't we making progress?'

'Yes, but at each step I see the confirmation of my first impressions. Behind all you've said, there must be something far more powerful than a simple puzzle about a film, even though that's important to you because of your profession. Your persistent visions must hide a troubled past.'

'But I don't remember any such thing!' insisted André, holding his hands out with the fingers spread, as if in a guarantee of good faith. 'There's nothing dark in my life. I would know it!'

'It might not affect you directly. You might simply be an unconscious witness to what he saw. I can't tell you any more at the moment. And it's not the scientific investigator who's speaking to you at the moment. I'm relying purely on my own instinct and experience. It's seldom a good idea to stir the ashes of the past. That's why I'm asking you the question for the last time: do you still wish to continue with our studies?'

The young author swallowed hard and looked straight ahead, as if at an imaginary object, before replying:

'Yes. *We have to.*'

5

THE CROSS

January 8, 1911

In the compartment of the local train which had left Charing Cross at precisely three minutes past seven, Cheryl Chapman watched the snow-covered Kentish countryside roll by. It was a pastoral scene which would normally have pleased her, particularly since she rarely left London. But her thoughts were elsewhere. She wondered why the only other occupant of the compartment hadn't attempted to strike up a conversation, even for courtesy's sake. Had he even noticed her presence? She was dressed to the nines, after all, with a perky pink hat adorned with flowers, set at a jaunty angle to accentuate her blonde hair and pert, mischievous features. At least, that's the impression she'd had of herself up to that point... But the brute opposite her seemed insensitive to her charms! Worse still, he'd only deigned to look at her boots, the least interesting part of her ensemble, for she had been unable to match the practical with the fashionable here in the countryside, where the wintry temperatures were well below those of the capital. Perhaps he hadn't dared look at her legs— or rather her knees, the only elements visible under her woollen skirt, as tightly fitting as her matching jacket? A man of experience, as he appeared to be, would surely have been able to assess the perfection of her anatomy at a single glance! But no, nothing. He hadn't uttered a single word since the jolting departure of the train. Surely she wasn't going to have to disrobe in order to get his attention! Yet when he'd abruptly opened the compartment door just before the departure, he had flashed her a warm but brief smile before asking whether there were any spare seats—a fact which was perfectly obvious, given that she was alone. But there had been no follow-up to the promising smile... And he'd even closed his eyes from time to time, even though he was seated directly opposite to her. The brief lapses allowed her to examine him at her leisure. He had to be over thirty, but gave the impression of being younger. His brown velvet suit wasn't new, but he wore it well. His aquiline nose gave him a rascally air without detracting from his charm. With his wavy black hair and dark features, he resembled the actor Henry Irving. But he looked tired. That must be it, Cheryl reassured herself: the morning after an over-indulgent night--that would explain his strange indifference.

As he opened his eyes and sat up, she turned to face the window. Out of the corner of her eye she saw him take a watch out of his waistcoat pocket. A beautiful gold watch which gleamed like the signet ring on her finger. She immediately thought of Andrew, who had one just like it. But the comparison between the two men stopped there. Even though they were of the same build, her current companion seemed more virile, more sure of himself....

Andrew... What was he to her, exactly? Not just her boss, for sure... Even though she had no doubts about his feelings for her, she was hard put to describe hers for him... Woman are so complicated, she thought in amusement, her eyes still riveted on the gleaming gold watch, when she realised her companion was smiling at her.

'You seem fascinated by my watch, madam.'

'Miss,' corrected Cheryl, kicking herself for having become lost in thought. 'I... I....' My goodness, why was she stammering? 'I have a friend, or rather an acquaintance, who has one just like it, and....'

'And I suppose he looks like me as well?' replied the other in a resonant voice, troubling to Cheryl's ears.

'No, not at all! You don't look at all like each other.'

Sinking into his seat and brushing back an unruly forelock, he replied in a relaxed, amused manner:

'I don't know whether to take that as a compliment or not. It doesn't matter. I'm Daren—and you?'

Cheryl was taken aback. He'd asked her for her first name, just like that? With no preliminaries? No, really, he was nothing like Andrew.

'Cheryl,' she stuttered automatically.

'Cheryl?' he replied, looking at her admiringly. 'That's a very pretty name, and it suits you, if you don't mind me saying so.'

The two occupants of the compartment stared at each other, their eyes wide open in stupefaction. There was a long moment of silence, interrupted only by the noise of the train.

'Cheryl?' he repeated. 'Would you, by any chance, be the Cheryl who works for the Sanders company?'

'And are you Daren, Victoria's brother?'

After a mutual acknowledgement, the two passengers burst out laughing. Five minutes later, they were chattering willy-nilly, just like old friends trying to catch up. They sensed a bond forming between them, which they knew could be explored at their leisure, given that they were destined to spend several days together under the same roof.

'Have you ever been to Raven Lodge?' asked Daren, rubbing his chin.

'No, never. This is the first time. I'm very indebted to your sister for having invited me.'

'You must be in her good books. She doesn't invite just anyone. In my case, it's a bit different... She feels somewhat obliged... Now let me guess: you're finding it hard to believe we're brother and sister?'

'It's true,' replied Cheryl with a smile. 'But I'd already been warned there was no resemblance.'

'I can't imagine what they've said about me. Those who are absent are always wrong. Isn't that what they say?'

'I make up my own mind,' declared Cheryl.

'Well, you'll have plenty of time. But I can tell you already that I'm not very complicated.'

He turned to contemplate the passing scenery.

'I'm happy anywhere,' he continued. 'I like the town, the country, the summer, the winter, the snow....'

'I love the snow as well!' exclaimed Cheryl, cheeks aglow with excitement.

'That's just as well, there's going to be plenty of it. Listen, I promised myself I'd take a little walk as soon as I arrived... After breakfast, of course. And, believe me, I'm hardly in top form. I passed a... let's just say I didn't sleep much. But I told myself that a dose of fresh air would do the trick. I'm the type who likes to take the bull by the horns.'

'So am I. And, believe me, I haven't had an easy life.'

'If you like, I can give you a tour of the surroundings.'

'You're on! Frankly, I was afraid I might be bored. But I could scarcely refuse an invitation from your sister.'

'Do you know Chandra?' asked Daren suddenly.

'Chandra, your sister's servant? Of course, he comes to the office frequently.'

'Of course. What was I thinking?' said Daren. 'He's not exactly the type to go unnoticed.'

'Why do you ask?'

'Because he's better than anyone else at preparing sumptuous breakfasts. He's generally in charge, to relieve the cook, who's already got her hands full... Even though we're not the best friends in the world, I know he has many qualities, and that's one of them. And I have to say that a couple of fried eggs, with sausages and a hot cup of tea, will do more for you than a roomful of doctors!

'I think we're here,' announced Cheryl, looking out of the window. 'This must be Broomfield. My, how time flies! It feels as though I only left London five minutes ago.'

It was eight o'clock by the time the carriage, pulled by a horse experiencing some difficulty in the snow, dropped them off in front of Raven Lodge. Whilst Daren paid the coachman, Cheryl looked around in wonder. The wide expanse of snow-covered fields, the surrounding woods, the imposing red-brick building standing out against the white background: everything looked marvellous. Daren, who was carrying the young woman's voluminous suitcase as well as his own travel bag, made his way to the entrance, pressed the door bell, and opened the door without waiting for a response. He entered a small, well-maintained panelled hallway, treading on the polished floor with his snow-covered shoes.

'Good morning, Chandra,' he bellowed as the servant appeared. 'How are you? In top form? We've got visitors. But I expect you knew that already. Let me introduce Miss Cheryl... Ah, of course, you've already met. Well, what is it?' he asked, noticing the disapproving look as the other looked down at the floor.

'Ah, yes,' continued Daren, turning round. 'I made a slight mess because of the damned snow. Be a good chap and bring us some slippers. After which you can take Miss Cheryl to her room whilst I freshen up in mine. Then you can prepare two of those delicious breakfasts for which you alone have the secret. Make sure they're ready in half an hour, because we're ravenous. And don't wake anyone else up for the time being. Miss Cheryl and I need to gather our strength before facing the hordes!'

At around nine o'clock, they left the house, well wrapped up and fully replenished by a breakfast which had lived up to all expectations. In the dining room they had only met Alice, who had dropped in briefly. If she'd been planning to have breakfast, she'd changed her mind, in order to leave the two of them alone. Her welcome was as frosty as the outside temperature. When asked whether her husband and Victoria were already up, her reply was a curt "no," upon which she'd left.

'She likes you about as much as she likes me,' observed Daren, rubbing his hands together.

'I suspect she's a bit jealous,' replied the young woman, looking down. 'But it's not a problem, I'm used to it.'

'I understand,' said Daren, turning towards his companion with an enigmatic smile. 'That's the first thought I had when I saw you on the train. Only pretty girls have that sort of problem.'

'You didn't let on at the time!'

'True, but I was in bad shape. I didn't feel up to a conversation worthy of the name. But I'm all right now! ' Taking her by the hand, he added: 'Let's go over there, towards the woods. If you like wide open spaces, as I do, you won't be disappointed.'

'Let's go!'

'The problem,' said Daren, looking round, 'is that there's quite a bit of mist. I'm not sure—.'

'No problem,' replied Cheryl gaily.

After a few false starts in the wooded space, which formed a crescent to the south of Raven Lodge, Daren declared triumphantly:

'Here we are! With all the snow and mist, it might be a little hard to make out, but we're now on the path to the cross.'

'The path to the cross?' repeated Cheryl, shivering before the wide expanse of snow, obscured here and there by patches of mist, 'I assume there must be a mysterious legend associated with it?'

'Of course. They say that three ogres terrorised any pilgrim who ventured there. Discretion prevents me from describing the gruesome details of what happened to them.'

So saying, Daren looked down in silence, as Cheryl came closer to him, shivering. He took her in his arms, then threw his head back in a guffaw:

'No! I'm teasing you. There's nothing but an old cross which gave its name to the path. And if you're afraid, be aware that was my intention....'

'Do you like making girls afraid?'

'No. I like to hold them in my arms!'

Whereupon he put his words into action. Cheryl let a few moments pass before reacting, then pulled away, more out of decency than anything else, for in truth she hadn't disliked the brief embrace. Then, mischievously, she pushed Daren over into the snow, which made him laugh.

'So, we're quits for the moment,' he said, getting up. 'Are you still ready to follow me?'

'Yes, but I'll be on the lookout,' she chuckled.

A few minutes later, the mist had thickened. As her footsteps crunched the snow, she heard her companion grumbling behind her.

'Is everything all right back there?' she asked.

'Yes, apart from the fact I just bumped into the damned cross.'

'You didn't see it?'

'Well, no. Thanks for warning me.'

'Listen, we're not alone... I think I can hear something... a dog barking.'

'That will be Alice taking Hector for a walk. It's her usual time... Have you met Hector? He's a nice doggie, ugly but very affectionate. That said, they're some way away, which is lucky, because the lovely Alice is beginning to tire me with her superior airs.'

'The lovely Alice? Is that what you think? Lovelier than I am?'

'Let me see... If I were to rate you on a scale of ten, from a purely physical point of view....'

'You'd have to see us nude for that! '

'You're right, of course. I'm prepared to wait for the opportunity, although in Alice's case I'm doubtful she'd co-operate. What's up, Cheryl?'

'Over there,' she replied, pointing to a dark shape lying in the snow. 'There's something. Or someone.'

She advanced cautiously, with Daren on her heels.

'My God!' she exclaimed. 'It's a woman. She looks as though she's dead. What happened to her? But, Daren,' she cried in a shrill voice, 'I think it's your sister!'

Her companion, who had stopped, perplexed, now advanced

resolutely in the snow, overtaking her. He knelt beside the prostrate woman, face down in the snow.

'I recognise her clothes. Very few people wear a violet coat.'

He leant over, pulling at a lock of hair, then letting it fall as if he'd touched a plague victim.

'It's her all right. And I fear the worst.'

He looked at the small hand sticking out from under the violet coat, and forced himself to hold it.

'It's frozen, and I can't feel anything. See for yourself.'

'She's dead, obviously,' said Cheryl, looking around. 'You can see clear footprints in the snow, coming from roughly the same direction we just took. What on earth happened to her?'

'There's blood on her hair.'

'Could she have fallen?' suggested Cheryl, leaning against her companion's shoulder.

'It's possible. It looks as though there's a bump in the snow, just next to her head... There must be a large stone there. But we'd better not touch anything and alert the others.'

'Yes,' agreed Cheryl soberly. 'And luckily there don't appear to be any other footprints than hers. Otherwise....'

'Yes?'

'Well, that might indicate more than a simple accident. And, with a personality like hers, I don't need to draw you a picture. Do you understand me, Daren?'

Her companion nodded sadly. Taking her hand, he said in a low voice:

'You'll see. This is all going to be laid at my door.'

6

THE UNKNOWN COLOUR

January 23, 1991

Carl Jelenski's mill, standing as it did at the top of a small hill adjacent to the village of Orville, constituted an excellent vantage point, not only to detect the arrival of the enemy, but also to observe the stars. Jelenski had astutely transformed the roof, adding movable flaps which allowed a powerful telescope to point up at the sky. The rest of the building had been judiciously decorated as well, in a cosy rustic manner with wooden panelling, white chalk walls and exposed rafters. The result was a half-timbered house which combined the aesthetic and the functional. Miscellaneous objects were scattered everywhere, in surprising harmony: old phonographs; terrestrial globes; ships' anchors; lanterns; maps of sea and sky; bookshelves full of esoteric works. Professor Jelenski was not just an academic, he was also a handyman with excellent taste.

Of medium height and stocky build, his ample grey hair made him look to be in his sixties, and his thick glasses under heavy brows made one irresistibly think of a curious owl. But he had a warm smile and gave no sign of suffering from boredom or solitude. After having listened to André's hesitant request and serving him a glass of port, he declared with a slight trace of foreign accent:

'You did the right thing in coming here, my boy. Christine gave you good advice. How is she, by the way?'

'Very well, as far as I know. But my wife is the one who really knows her. Let's just say they share a common passion for flowers.'

'And gossip, just like every woman,' replied the other, with a knowing wink. 'I like to do so as well, but it's often to myself, by force of circumstance. What I suggest is that you snuggle down comfortably between those two stuffed crows and explain your problem in detail, in such a way as I can understand how I may help.'

After describing what he wanted, André felt relaxed, as if relieved of a burden. Although Célia had doubted the usefulness of talking to the astronomer, he had felt that any help would be better than none. And he wasn't sorry he'd come. Carl Jelenski was a sympathetic individual, with an original and interesting turn of mind. At the very least he would make a good fictional character for André's next book.

'... and, according to Dr. Moreau,' he concluded, 'it's necessary to determine whether it's the identification of the film which is of prime importance, or the "images" which might be connected to some distant personal memory.'

'And what do you think?'

'Finding the film is of the highest priority.'

'You're both right!' declared Jelenski gaily. 'You can't have one without the other. Seeing the film again will clarify matters, and will bring you peace of mind, even at the suggestion of a troubled past. I certainly haven't got Dr. Moreau's expertise in the subject, but notions of the past and of time are a bit of a speciality of mine. Speaking of time, I mean time passing... How can I put it? I get to see it on every occasion I perform an observation. Time is of vital importance in everything. For example, when I look at you I see the past. By the time your image reaches my brain, it's already past. In that example, the delay is infinitesimal, but when I look at the stars it's a matter of light-years. When I look at a star, I see a past already millions of years old... Do you see the importance now? And what more representative than a watch, better still a gold one, to signify its eminently precious character?'

'I understand... So do you believe in the symbolic aspect of the watch? Could my mind have been influenced for that reason?'

'Perhaps not uniquely. I was merely trying to stress the importance of time, in your case as in everything. For us astronomers, the notion of time is often confused with that of space, if only because of their infinite character. Besides, our universe, with its myriads of planets, stars, and galaxies, is nothing but a gigantic mechanical clock mechanism. Each element gravitates around another, executing slow rotations in space in a sort of cunningly orchestrated ballet, all linked by filaments of light, by which I mean each beam, each reflection of a star visible from another point in space.'

André, perplexed, rubbed his neck and observed:

'A spider's web, in other words, made from filaments of light?'

44

'If you like, but in three dimensions.' Then he added, with a knowing smile: 'Spider's web, gold watch, we function by symbols. And, from a dramatic author as well-known as you, with your imagination, it's hardly surprising. Not to mention your spiral staircase, which could be a representation of the infinite, or of madness.'

'So one should beware of symbols?'

'Yes and no. Because at the same time, they can be very precious. They can sometimes lead us astray, but they often reveal the truth. But I'm afraid I've confused you with all those scientific notions. Nevertheless, I think I can help you.'

***

Standing in front of her mirror, clothed in bits of material hurriedly assembled, Célia observed her reflection with a critical air. Was her *contrapposto* too pronounced? Her slit dress certainly emphasised the grace of her silhouette, but it must not be exaggerated and run the risk of being too alluring. She asked advice from her husband, standing by the side of the mirror, armed with a camera.

He was in the habit of watching his wife work. There was nothing like a snapshot to inspire him in his sketches. And the role didn't displease him at all. It was already past ten o'clock at night; two small projectors, placed apart, highlighted Célia's subtle form, and André scarcely thought about his afternoon session with the astronomer. In his role of technician, he was adjusting the frame of the shots.

'It's perfect,' he said. 'Don't move. Watch the dicky-bird.'

After several more shots, Célia exchanged her attire for her dressing gown. She lit a cigarette and gave her husband a perfunctory "thank you."

'Not at all,' replied André, 'but I hope to be paid in return.'

Célia didn't respond. She remarked casually:

'By the way, Dr. Moreau dropped by in the late afternoon, whilst you were still with your astrologer.'

'Astronomer,' André corrected her.

'In fact, you haven't said anything about it. How did it go?'

'I don't really know how to describe it,' he replied. 'It was rather strange.' His voice suddenly changed: 'What? Dr. Moreau dropped by? What did he want?'

'He brought two video cassettes.'

'And you're only telling me now?'

'Yes. I wanted you to concentrate on our photo session.'

'Where are they?'

'In the drawing room, next to the television. You can leave, I don't need you any more,' she said, extending a beautifully shaped leg illuminated by the projectors. 'Just make sure you don't break a leg on the way.'

A few moments later, André nervously introduced a cassette into the player. On it someone had written, with a black felt pen "Sorry, Wrong Number—Litvak, 1948." As the suggestive music started to play, he turned the light off and settled down in the armchair. An observer could have followed the images of the film reflected in his eyes, widened by a curious mixture of impatience and agony. An hour and a half later, the words "The End" appeared, accompanied by the final chords. Célia appeared at that very moment, having cautiously opened the door.

'Well, darling?' she asked apprehensively.

'Well,' he repeated, in a clear voice. 'It wasn't bad. Not bad at all. Burt Lancaster was his usual self, as was Barbara Stanwyck—that's to say sublime. She's just as good whether she's playing a dangerous woman or a terrified one. *But it wasn't that.*'

'I didn't think so, darling.'

'Neither did I. It was the least likely.'

'I took a quick look at the other one earlier, just a few scenes in fast forward... I don't want to raise your hopes too much, but it seems quite promising and quite close to your description. I don't know whether I'll be in bed by the time you've finished, because I have a couple of things more to finish. So I'll leave you, you don't need me any more.'

'Good idea,' he said, after the door closed behind his wife.

He got up and served himself a whisky, which he placed on the table next to the armchair, next to a packet of cigarettes and a half-full ashtray. He placed *The Spiral Staircase* into the machine. At the sounds of the opening chords he sensed a shiver run through him. And the feeling didn't lessen as he watched. On the contrary. The story was as frightening as one could wish for, the camera shots were sublime, and the shadows expertly placed. It was very reminiscent of German expressionism. Siodmak, the director, was obviously from that school. One after the other he noticed the critical themes he'd noted in the list he'd given to Dr. Moreau. A menacing house; the black grill of the gate, made white by lightning and driving rain; doors creaking as they slowly opened; the shadow of a murderer clad all in black; and the faces of frightened women. It was almost a festival. There was no gold watch, but that didn't matter, because that element had become less certain. And the key fished out of a puddle was troubling. Above all, there was that spiral staircase, omnipresent, haunting and looking like a passage to hell. The only problem was that it was black, not white. And he was certain, in his memory, that it was white. And much narrower than the one in the film. And it didn't go down to a cellar, but up to the landing of a solidly built house. He could have believed all the rest corresponded to his memories, but not the staircase. And he hadn't seen the close-up of a door handle turning slowly.

When he went very late into his wife's workshop, she raised her eyes from a fashion plate and pulled a face:

'Something tells me it wasn't the one.'

'Right. I was so close to believing, but there were a couple of insurmountable details. I'm very disappointed, to say the least.'

'There's still a third film, isn't there?'

'Yes, but I've stopped believing, darling. It would be too much to expect to find it now. I had too much hope of seeing that film again. And I know that a wish which is too fervent never happens.'

'I can remember you talking about something you wished for more than anything it the world, which eventually was yours.'

'Ah?' he replied in surprise. 'Ah, yes, it's true,' he added with a tender smile. '*You*, darling.'

He kissed her gently on the cheek.

'You see,' she continued, 'everything comes to him who waits. And you still haven't told me about your session this afternoon.'

'That also started out very promisingly,' he replied, after suppressing a yawn. 'I was very impressed by the old mill, very well restored, and by its owner, who is clearly competent in his chosen field, the study of the sky and the stars. But later, when he showed me a crumpled old manuscript, left to him by an archaeologist friend, who is supposed to have made a fabulous discovery in an Amazonian grotto about an unknown colour, I started to have doubts. And when he told me it allowed him to see "the invisible," images of the past or who knows what... I started to have serious doubts about his mental stability. And when he talked about madness being often symbolised by a spiral staircase, I could have sworn he was talking about his own particular case!'

'Christine led me to believe that he had a gift,' said Célia thoughtfully. 'That he saw things others missed. And that she'd had the opportunity to verify it.'

'That may be. I'm willing to believe in the gifts of some mediums. I've read a lot of troubling testimony to that effect. But that story about an unknown and magical colour is a bit hard to swallow.'

'Maybe. But this fellow is beginning to interest me.'

'Ah? Have you changed your mind?'

'Maybe,' she replied, with a sphinx-like smile. 'His accent, his mysterious origins, his past which nobody seems to know anything about....'

'Hmm. Looks to me as though you've got an idea at the back of your mind.'

'Well we definitely need to know more about him. I'll start by questioning Christine. And you, you'd better see him again.'

'I suppose so,' he said, unconvinced. 'I'll be happy to listen to his rantings again. But, as far as the film goes, I put more faith in good old Dr. Moreau. And I hope he manages to lay his hands on that impossible-to-find *The Unseen*.'

7

THE KING IN YELLOW

Narrative of Achilles Stock

January 9, 1911

Bouncing around in the carriage taking us to Broomfield, Owen Burns and I inhaled the refreshing air of the countryside on that January Monday. Despite all the bumps, my friend managed to conserve his dignity. He was a man of confident bearing, approaching--as was your humble servant--the forty-year mark. His drooping eyelids gave him a false air of indolence, whereas in fact his eyes gleamed with alertness and intelligence. My frequent readers are fully aware of his astonishing faculties, which have enabled him to solve numerous cases which were baffling Scotland Yard, and his rather special character, which this tale will expose even further. I myself was a South African peasant, some of whose corners had been smoothed by contact with the English soil—I emigrated just before the turn of the century—and who had been civilised by the frequent company of my friend since that date. At least that, I sensed, was his opinion of me. The quick trip to Kent had been decided the previous evening, when Owen had received a telegram from Inspector Wedekind, who, in the tersest telegraphic style, had asked for his assistance with a case of ostensible suicide which had all the appearance of a perfect crime in the snow.

A perfect crime in the snow... The mere mention of those words was enough for Owen to make a decision and transform him from languid boredom into the sparkling form which only occurred when he was in love or grappling with a mysterious crime. Added to which, crimes in the snow were something of a speciality. The reader will recall *The Lord of Misrule, The Flower Girl,* and *The Wolf of Fenrir,* amongst others.

The way in which he spoke of the beauty of the countryside and the majestic luminosity of the snow spoke volumes about his state of mind. A few minutes later, the carriage drew up at Raven Lodge, an imposing Georgian building, where a uniformed police officer was awaiting us. Shortly thereafter, we were passing through some woods and crossing a vast expanse of snow in the company of Inspector Wedekind, pausing on the way to observe an old cross, before arriving at a spot where the snow had been tamped down and marked with a stake.

'It hasn't snowed since, which is a bit of luck,' declared Wedekind, who was in his fifties, with bushy eyebrows and a thick moustache. 'This is where the body of Victoria Sanders was found yesterday morning. She was the director of the firm by the same name, which specialises in the import of fine fabrics, and she leaves a substantial inheritance.'

'I know of Victoria Sanders,' remarked Owen, stretching his hand up into the air. 'A wealthy woman of excellent taste, which is not necessarily a contradiction.'

'In that case, I'll run through the basic facts in chronological order.'

'I'd be obliged.'

The inspector took a notebook out of his coat and thumbed through it:

'First, a few words by way of context. Mrs. Sanders had invited a number of people close to her for a long weekend: her brother Daren Bellamy; the deputy director of the firm, Andrew Johnson, and his wife Alice; his private secretary, Cheryl Chapman; and servant and confidant, Chandra Ganesh. For the occasion, she had engaged the services of Mr. and Mrs. Benson from Broomfield as handyman and cook respectively. They looked after the house when the owner was absent.

'It all starts on Saturday night, or rather Sunday morning—yesterday, that is—at about two o'clock in the morning. Mr. and Mrs. Johnson hear a loud cry in the house. Mrs. Alice gets up and finds a very disturbed Victoria in the corridor. She's just had a nightmare and is about to go out for some fresh air to calm herself down. Mrs. Alice goes back to bed. It's around that time that the snow stops. At around seven o'clock that same morning, Daren Bellamy and Cheryl

50

Chapman take the train from Charing Cross to Broomfield. Daren had, in fact, left Broomfield that Saturday to go to a party in London, where he had spent the night. Miss Cheryl was coming to Raven Lodge for the first time. They had never met before, but make acquaintance in the train. That may seem a bit odd , but you'll understand better when you see them, particularly him. At about nine o'clock, our two freshly-minted friends take a little walk here to enjoy the charm of the countryside... before discovering the body of Victoria Sanders here. According to the medical examiner, she probably died at around four o'clock that morning. That's yet to be confirmed, but he's pretty confident.'

'I see,' said Owen, adjusting his thick woollen scarf. 'I presume you're about to describe the footprints in the snow in some detail?'

'Yes,' said the inspector, shooting him a sharp glance, 'and that's where it gets complicated. But let me finish with the cause of death, a violent blow to the temple, either from a blunt instrument, or by falling on the large stone you see there, where the body's head was positioned. We've brushed the snow away to make it more visible.'

'Hmm,' murmured Owen, stepping forward. 'Falling onto that whilst walking is really unlucky.'

'You can say that again. Frankly, I don't believe that explanation, even if the evidence points to it. But let's go back to the footprints. I realise the area has been scuffled by my men, but we've tried to preserve, to the extent possible, the footprints of the witnesses and the victim. The snow here is at least six inches thick and has a nice, firm surface. The prints left by the victim start from the woods near the property and lead directly to where the body was found. According to our expert, they are of someone walking normally, neither running nor dragging their feet.'

'That seems to be right,' agreed Owen, 'according to the even spacing between the steps.'

'Furthermore, they're definitely those of the victim, who was wearing ankle-boots. The prints are very clear. And, taking into account the snow, which started at around ten in the evening and lasted until around two in the morning, we can deduce with certainty that Mrs. Sanders came here following her nightmare—let's say between three and five in the morning—prior to her fatal fall.

PLAN OF RAVEN LODGE AND SURROUNDING AREA

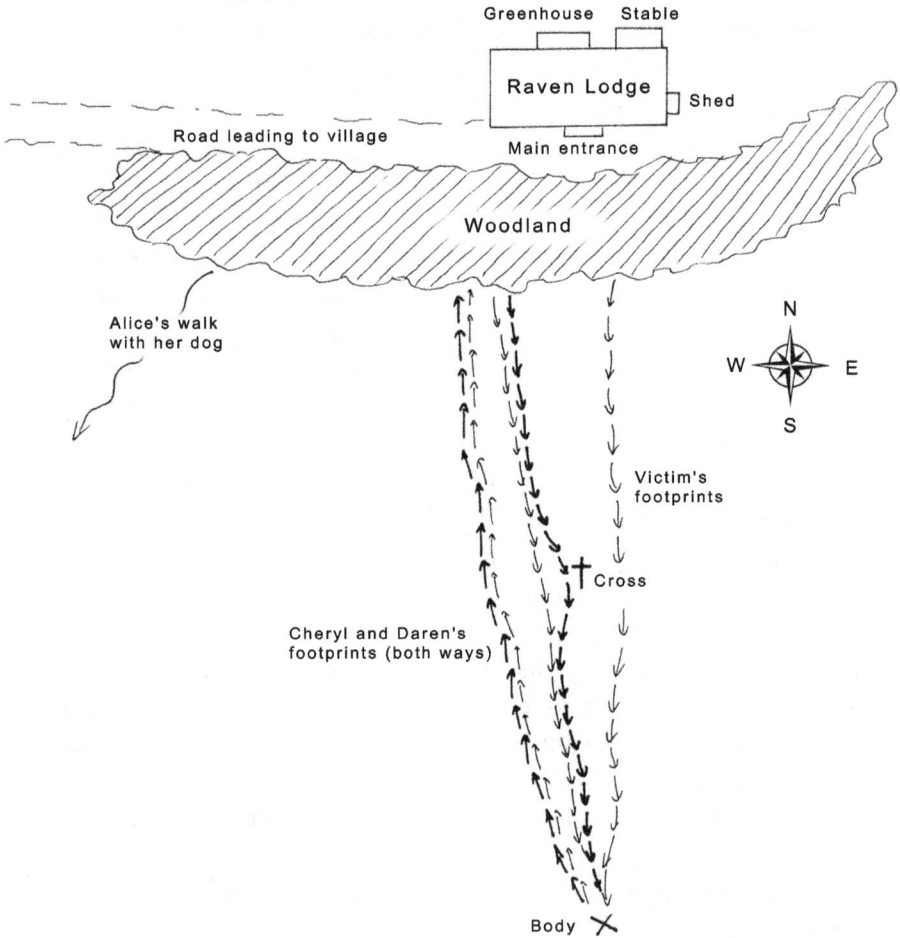

Greenhouse   Stable

Raven Lodge   Shed

Road leading to village

Main entrance

Woodland

Alice's walk
with her dog

N

W   E

S

Victim's
footprints

Cross

Cheryl and Daren's
footprints (both ways)

Body X

'Unfortunately, it's impossible to determine her movements near the entrance to the house and the access road, which is sheltered by the woods to some degree. Around there, any traces have been obliterated by walkers or vehicles. And inside the woods there are several areas completely free of snow. The path taken by Mrs. Sanders is vague and discontinuous, just like that of Daren and Cheryl, who obviously fumbled around before striking out on the snow. Similarly for Alice Johnson when she walked her dog, who ran about all over the place.

'By contrast, the prints from the woods to here, across the wide stretch of snow, are perfectly clear. The prints left by Daren and Cheryl, here and back, are more or less parallel to those of the victim. Or, rather, they converge, because hers start about fifty yards to the east of theirs. And, as you can see, it's about three hundred yards from the woods to here, or about a five-minute walk.

'The prints made by the couple have been closely examined as well. There's nothing suspect about them, just like the victim's. They match the boots they were wearing, and our expert has determined that there's no difference between the depth on the way here and the depth on the way back, and he's the Yard's top specialist. There was a bit of scuffling around the body, but that's understandable. To sum it up, between the woods and here there three sets of prints: those of Mrs. Sanders one way and those of Daren and Cheryl in both directions. And they're the only ones we've found in a range of a hundred yards!'

Owen nodded thoughtfully, then bent down for a closer examination.

'I must admit I can't find anything suspect, either,' he declared eventually. 'And you will know, if you have taken the trouble to read my monograph on the subject, that I am far from an amateur on the subject. And, all around, nothing? Not even fox traces?'

'Nothing. There were some of Alice and her dog, but they were much farther away, more then a hundred yards to the west.'

'More than a hundred yards? That would make murder at a distance rather difficult,' observed Owen jokingly. 'Really, inspector, other than an accident, or suicide in the extreme case, I can't see what else it could be.'

So saying, he decided to retrace his steps in order to get a broader view of the footprints. Those of Cheryl and Daren ran relatively parallel and close, except for the cross in the outward direction. The man's prints passed just in front of it, whereas the woman's were ten yards away. The twin sets of prints were farther to the west on the way back.

'I can confirm that your expert was correct in his verdict. There's nothing abnormal about these prints.'

'So Mrs. Sanders just had an unlucky fall,' growled the policeman. 'The problem is that she was very rich, and her brother, who has a toxic reputation, is going to inherit quite a packet.'

'But wasn't he in London when the tragedy occurred? Both he and Miss Cheryl?'

'I haven't had time to examine their alibis carefully,' grumbled Wedekind, 'but you can be sure I will.'

'If they left London at seven in the morning, that's hardly enough time to have committed the murder in the middle of the night. Not impossible if it occurred at four in the morning, but still....'

Arriving at Raven Lodge, we made our way round the building, starting from the east side, where a lean-to shed protected the reserves of wood. Here, too, any footprints in the snow had been scuffed over. Owen gave the logs a cursory look and tried to turn the handle of a service door without success. At the rear of the building were a disused stable and a greenhouse, in which Owen could see, to his astonishment, several potted plants, all of the same variety and carefully aligned. Whilst he was inspecting them through the glass, Wedekind said pointedly that botanical questions were not the priority of the hour.

'Art is always a priority,' retorted Owen. 'But tell me, Wedekind, have you searched the victim's room?'

'Of course, Burns. What do you take me for?'

'Anything in particular to report?'

'No,' said the policeman, stroking his moustache. 'No traces of blood, no strange objects... just some business about a book that had disappeared. In fact, disappeared is too big a word. Mrs. Sanders could have left it anywhere, between the moment it was seen on her bedside table the night of the drama, to when we inspected the room the following afternoon.'

'A disappearing book,' said my friend with a smile, 'that's strange. What do you think, Achilles?'

'Well,' I replied, caught by surprise, 'books have always been... I mean "show me what you read and I'll show you who you are."'

'Very good, Achilles,' said Owen, patting me on the shoulder. 'I like people who speak wittingly. You haven't said anything for a while, to the point that I was wondering about the usefulness of our relationship. A book, then, Wedekind, but which one? I hope you've made a note of it.'

'Let's see. Let me think. There was "yellow" in the title... The princess, the prince... No, it was the king, *The King in Yellow.*'

Owen Burns froze suddenly, as if struck by lightning. Eyes bulging, he stared at the policeman:

'*The King in Yellow?*', he asked forcefully. 'Mrs. Sanders was reading *The King in Yellow* a few hours before she had a terrible nightmare and met her end?'

'It would seem so.'

'And you've only just told me?'

'So what?' stammered Wedekind, like a child being criticised by his teacher.

'So, *it can't have been a coincidence!*'

'I'm afraid I don't understand.'

'It means that Mrs. Sanders' fall can't have been accidental!'

8

THE STRANGE LOOK

June 27, 1991

'Yes, Mr. Jelenski did speak about himself, but only in snatches, never anything precise,' said Christine in her soft voice.

She was sitting on her terrace in a wicker chair, protected from the hot sun of the late-June afternoon by the shadows of an arbour completely invaded by a Virginia creeper.

Christine's house was more modest than hers, thought Célia, seated opposite her hostess, but it was more rustic and intimate. The two cats lying lazily in a corner, next to a number of potted plants, were a testimony to the serenity of the place.

'But he does seem to have led a complicated life before settling in France a while ago,' she continued. 'I think he's Polish, although I'm not sure, and his parents moved country several times. He told me about his mother, who had a very unhappy childhood. She was Ukrainian and lost her entire family in the famine which ravaged the country at the start of the thirties. And he completed some of his studies in Berlin. That's about all I know. You'll have to ask him yourself, I think.'

'It's always rather delicate,' replied Célia, after clearing her throat. 'Particularly since I hardly know him. We've only seen each other in the village.'

'But your husband went to see him, didn't he?'

'Yes. He was highly impressed by his knowledge, and he's indebted to you for having effected the introduction. But....'

'But?' repeated Christine mischievously.

'Well, he wonders if... how to put it?... if he isn't somewhat affected by his solitude.'

'I understand. He thinks Carl is a bit of a crank!'

'A little bit, yes. Apparently he went a bit far with his theories about the past, or his visions of the future, or something like that.'

'I can put myself in your position,' said Christine. 'Even more so because I had the same impression at first. But he proved himself on two occasions. It's not easy to talk about them because they involve very personal situations.' She gave a deep sigh. 'But I can tell you this much: a few years ago I was a baby-sitter looking after a little boy who was almost like a son to me. He drowned accidentally in a neighbour's pool. I was desolate. Because the incident occurred at night, the circumstances were never clearly established. One day I talked to Carl about it.'

'And he was able to tell you what happened!'

'Exactly. He said it was nothing more than the night-time escapade of a child burning with curiosity, and that relieved me greatly. Even today I visit his grave—you must have noticed that I'm away often.'

'My sympathies. But how do you know his explanation was the right one?'

'Because he talked about details he could not have known. The kid was never without his favourite toy, a little stuffed duck, which was found beside him in the pool.'

'Disconcerting,' said Célia, after a brief silence. 'To be frank, I tend to be sceptical by nature, but my husband and I were witnesses to another extraordinary event, after which we asked ourselves some serious questions about the mysteries of life.'

And she proceeded to describe the episode of the matching seashells and its effect on their lives.

'But that's wonderful!' exclaimed Christine. 'I've seldom heard such a beautiful story. You're guaranteed a happy life. And, by the way, it shows. I've always felt there was a deep bond between you.'

'A deep bond, yes, but we don't always share the same objectives.'

'So much the better,' replied Christine. 'Harmony is a wise mixture of opposites, not the juxtaposition of identical elements. Your personal development is a pleasure to see. You're very lucky, very few of us can say as much. Speaking personally, I have no complaints. I've had a few setbacks, but a lot of good things have happened. But as to my personal development....'

She stroked the multi-coloured scarf around her neck before continuing:

'I've always loved to sing, and dreamt of being a great opera performer. But I had my tonsils removed, and for some reason it affected my voice. No one knows why; I'm a mystery to science. But not only did my voice change, I catch cold at the first breeze, and my dreams have gone up in smoke.'

'That's terribly sad,' said Célia. 'But perhaps it was destiny.'

'That's what I always told myself,' sighed Christine. 'As Carl would say, it was written in the stars,' she added, with a smile.

'Speaking of whom,' asked Célia, 'when did Carl arrive here in the village?'

'Seven or eight years ago, to the best of my knowledge.'

'So, at about the same time as you?'

'Yes. It was the same year, now I think about it.'

'And Dr. Moreau?'

'He came quite a bit later. He bought his house three years ago, just before retiring. By the way, how's it going with your husband?'

'Quite well, I'd say. He continues to see him regularly. There was a slight disappointment the other day, after he thought he'd been successful. But I'm sure it's just a temporary setback. Dr. Moreau seems to know what he's doing.'

***

The blue elephant in Dr. Moreau's drawing room was once again subject to an attentive examination. It was even beginning to haunt André's dreams. It had become his introspective companion; a familiar figure giving out pale blue reflections in the dim light.

'It's just a near miss,' declared Dr. Moreau with a calm assurance. 'It's rare to find success on the first try. And we can already eliminate two "suspects," so we are progressing, slowly but surely.'

'And what news of the third "suspect"?'

'None for the moment. I told you that Lewis Allen's *The Unseen* was very rare. That said, I have what might be good news. Do you remember telling me that Siodmak's *The Spiral Staircase* had an atmosphere very similar to your unknown film?'

'Yes, and I might almost add "alas!" because I had high hopes for a while. But I'm quite sure it wasn't.'

'Well, by a strange coincidence, *The Unseen* is based on a story by an English writer, Ethel Lina White, who also wrote *The Spiral Staircase*. I know it's only a coincidence, but I must admit to experiencing a slight thrill when my correspondent told me. It's a good omen, isn't it? At least I hope it will start you off on the right foot.'

Once again, André ensconced himself in the sofa and recounted his distant memories, always the same images: the black grill of the gate; the driving rain; the doorknob; the great spiral staircase with its interminable banister... The terrified face of the woman about to scream.

'Just a moment,' cut in Dr. Moreau, with unaccustomed rudeness. 'That face, that terror... I get the impression that's what's left the deepest impression.'

'It's possible. That's the most obvious expression of fear.'

'A question: were you alone when you watched the trailer? Alone in the room in front of the television next to the large green plant? Alone, or with your friend Guy? Try to remember, it could be important.'

'I wasn't alone. There was someone else there, but it wasn't Guy. I think it was that woman Rita. Black hair, violet dress, gold jewellery. She was sitting next to me, watching as well.'

'Her face. Do you remember her face?'

'Yes, she had a look on her face like the woman in the film. Her eyes were wide open, and her mouth as well.'

André gave a long sigh and buried his head in his hands, before adding:

'It's incredible. In those last few moments I saw her as clearly as if it were yesterday.'

'That woman made an impression on you, there's no doubt about it. You've given a very detailed description of her. Not only did you, as an adolescent, become unconsciously aware of her sensuality, but her fear also affected you. And it's that, in addition to the images, which burnt that film sequence into your memory.'

'It—it's possible. I can almost feel that "violet" physical presence next to me.'

'Who communicated her fear. The fear which has left such a deep impression, and which makes you shiver even now.'

André passed a hand across his moist forehead.

'There's something else I want to tell you about, which involves the gold watch. You may be right that it's not directly related to the film.

If you remember, I told you about M. Lamblin's quick-tempered nature. I recently remembered a stormy scene between him and his wife, when she was still alive. She owned a gold watch, which she complained had never worked. In her exasperation, after several futile attempts at repair, she told some friends at dinner that she was ready to get rid of it. Someone offered to take it off her hands and she felt obliged to give it to them, a gesture which she bitterly regretted later. I wasn't present during the quarrel, but apparently she brought it up. M. Lamblin said it served her right and it all ended in tears. It stuck in my mind because I felt embarrassed, as did my friend Guy. I didn't know then who had taken the watch, but now I think about it, the aforementioned Rita might have worn it as a sort of medallion. A bright shining watch over her violet dress, just like her bracelets.'

'I warned you, André,' declared the psychoanalyst sententiously. 'We're engaged in a troubled past, and I'm afraid we've gone too far for you to turn back. I've sensed from the beginning that there was more than a film behind your obsession. I even wondered whether it could be a case of metempsychosis, reincarnation of the soul, and whether you were reliving a previous life. I'm pretty sceptical on the subject, but I can't ignore certain papers on the subject by eminent colleagues. You evoked your memories with such passion, such fervour, it was clear it was more than just a simple puzzle. The truth lay elsewhere. Your acute sensitivity picked up the scent of your neighbour's fear, her guilty conscience, the horror of a past event provoked whilst watching, with you, images which carried a deep significance for her.'

'So you think she must have been implicated in something serious?'

'There's no doubt about it. Otherwise why would an adult female react with such an expression of terror to a detective film? Incidentally, I'm willing to bet that the television didn't break down the next day by accident. A malicious hand, on the pretext of watering the adjacent plant, must have sprayed water on it. And no guesses as to whose hand. Those images must have recalled something shameful.'

'A murder... as in the film?'

'It seems highly likely. If you still insist on playing the detective of the past, I strongly encourage you to locate her and her brother Heinrich.'

61

'That's all very well, but where would I find them today?' the playwright asked himself, stroking his chin. 'By my calculations, the events occurred twenty-five years ago and they must be over sixty by now. So they've probably retired to somewhere quiet, if they're still alive. Hmm, it's not going to be easy and I don't even know where to start. Particularly since, on the Lamblin side, there aren't many left. Guy died in an accident several years later. Now I think about it, that's all the more reason to find that film!'

'I couldn't agree with you more,' agreed the psychoanalyst. 'It's connected to a real-life drama, if only because of the images. Images which could prove very revealing. We'll have to redouble our efforts. I'll find the film and you find Rita!'

9

ALICE AND ANDREW

Narrative of Achilles Stock (continued)

At around three o'clock, we gathered in the drawing room of Raven Lodge to listen to our first witness, who was waiting for us already, ensconced in one of the couches. Wedekind introduced Alice Johnson, whom he said was the last person to have talked to the victim. Owen seemed immediately smitten by Mrs. Johnson, who was a very pretty woman, I must admit. His eyes went from her hands to a lace mat near her on the sofa, and back to her hands again.

Intrigued, she asked:

'Is there anything wrong, sir?'

'Not at all. Please excuse me, I was simply admiring your hands, saying to myself that such pretty hands should only be devoted to pretty things—such as the exquisite embroidery I see there. In that, you remind me of a very dear friend.'

It was a reference to *The Lord of Misrule*, which I have already mentioned, but shall not dwell on here. Alice Johnson hesitated before replying:

'Well, sir, I'm flattered by your interest in my hands.'

I could see that a spark had passed between them. For a moment I had feared a different reaction. Unless I had been hoping to see Owen taken down a peg and lose his insufferable self-confidence.

'And flattered that you find them my most important feature,' she added with a note of irony.

Fearing a too risqué reply from my friend, Wedekind intervened:

'I think it would be appropriate to talk of matters that interest us, Burns.'

'Art is the only matter of interest here, and the hand is the primary instrument of every artist, be they painter, musician or writer. That said, we're all ears, madam. Perhaps you could start with Mrs. Sanders' nightmare, being as precise as possible as to the details.'

'I shall try. But first, I'd like to say that I saw Mrs. Sanders here in this room at the end of the evening and she seemed to be her normal self, relaxed and self-assured. Perhaps vaguely preoccupied with her brother, but that was all. I say that because she made a remark about him never changing. She left to go to bed, and Andrew and I followed her shortly thereafter. Our room, like hers, is upstairs. At two o'clock in the morning, I was awakened by a loud cry.'

Alice stopped to purse her lips, then went on:

'Well, more or less. By that I mean that I, too was in the midst of a dream. I don't know if that's of any importance....'

'Everything is important,' replied Owen. 'Don't leave out any detail, if you please.'

'Very well. I saw the door knob of our room turn slowly—very slowly—as if someone was trying to get in without making any noise.' Her eyes widened, as if reliving a frightening moment. 'So I got out of bed and put my back against the door... and saw the knob continue to turn. Then I felt pressure on the door... It was horrible. I don't know how long I stayed there, with my heart beating as if to burst... Then I went back to bed. And that was when I woke up and heard the cries.'

'And are you sure you were dreaming about the door knob?'

'Yes. Well, maybe not right then. As you know, when you have a nightmare it actually feels very real at the time. But I thought so later. It would have been very difficult in the darkness to have seen the knob move. And I must confess I've been subject to nightmares quite often since that terrible accident. Perhaps you remember the train that was derailed last October, on the Leeds line?'

'Of course,' replied Owen. 'It was a terrible tragedy.'

'Well, I was one of those who escaped. It was a dreadful experience I wouldn't wish on anyone, even though I've now recovered. Where was I... Yes, as I was saying, I heard cries at two o'clock.'

'How can you be so sure of the hour?'

'Andrew and I looked at the bedside clock. Which is what convinced my husband to stay in bed, I have to say. I tried to shame him but in vain, which got me a bit upset. Eventually, I put on my dressing-gown and went out to look for myself. I saw Mrs. Sanders come out of her room and head in the direction of the stairs. She was dressed as if she was going out. I caught up to her and asked her if everything was all right. Her eyes were bloodshot and she explained that she'd just had a terrible nightmare. She'd decided to go out and get some fresh air. I tried to dissuade her by pointing out that it wasn't wise to go out in all that snow. She replied that the snow was tapering off, which was true. At that point we were in the kitchen. I couldn't really go against her will. She'd told me everything was all right and it was simply a nightmare. I went back upstairs and left her there, without thinking for a moment that it would be the last time I'd see her alive.'

'Did she tell you about her nightmare?'

'No, but I didn't ask.'

'Very well, and afterwards?'

'I went back to bed, quite miffed about Andrew's laziness. He went to get me a glass of milk, no doubt in order to pacify me, after which I went back to sleep right away. I woke up at eight o'clock. Chandra was already in the kitchen. He's the one who takes care of service at that hour. The Bensons go back to the village every night and don't get here until after nine. Because Mrs. Sanders doesn't get up at a specific time, we weren't concerned about her absence. Her brother and Miss Cheryl arrived soon afterwards. Chandra took care of them. I wasn't in any particular hurry to talk to them. I saw them in the kitchen a little later, around a quarter to nine, then I went to take Hector, our dog, for a walk. I got back a good half hour later. The Bensons had just arrived. That's when I learnt the tragic news.'

'Did you know the victim well?' asked Owen, who had lit a cigar and was blowing perfect smoke rings in the direction of the ceiling.

'Less than my husband, of course. Let's say we were on good terms, nothing more. I have to say she wasn't a cheerful and expansive sort. She was very strict and demanding of her employees. But, deep down, I think she hid behind an outer shell of tough businesswoman. Occasionally one could spot her weaknesses. Her artistic sensitivity, for example. She was passionate about her profession and about the quality of her products, and not just because of the profits they brought in. Or the idea of this invitation, to get to know each other and foster the team spirit. But from that point of view it wasn't a success, mainly because of her brother.'

'And what do you think of him? Is he like his sister?'

Alice Johnson stiffened before replying:

'Absolutely not. He's almost her opposite. He's not a gentleman, and I don't like his manners. But we aren't all of that opinion. Miss Cheryl seems to appreciate him.'

'Miss Cheryl Chapman,' said Owen. 'Let me see, she's your husband's secretary isn't she?'

The hard expression which came into Alice's eyes was impossible not to notice.

'Amongst other things. To give you some idea, she posed nude for him in the past. Which I only discovered recently, I may add.'

She described the episode of the painting, which Wedekind had already briefed us about.

'But for more information about the origins of the portrait,' she concluded, 'please address your questions to the interested parties. As for me, I've never had a clear explanation from my husband and even less from his model.'

Owen nodded, then asked:

'Getting back to Mrs. Sanders, what do you think could have happened to her that night?'

'It all seems fairly clear to me. She went out to get some fresh air, despite my advice, and took a walk in the snow—no doubt still under the influence of her bad dream, dazed and unsteady—before having a bad fall.'

'If things had been as clear as that, madam, we wouldn't be here.'

'I understand, but I can't see any other explanation.'

'The time of death is estimated at around four o'clock. But you left her much earlier than that, didn't you?'

'Yes, it must have been a quarter past two or a little later.'

'So she waited alone in the kitchen for over an hour before deciding to go out?'

Alice made a gesture of ignorance, then suggested:

'Unless she went back up to her room for a while? I couldn't tell you, my husband and I were already sound asleep.'

'Very well, let's leave that aside for the moment and talk about the famous painting.'

'I've said everything I have to say about that,' she retorted, stiffening.

'I wanted to talk about the moment that you and your husband went into Mrs. Sanders' room. You've been very clear up until now, madam, and I'm obliged to you for it, but I'm now going to ask you to be even more precise, because this is a critical point, perhaps the most crucial of all.'

'I'm listening,' she replied, raising a quizzical eyebrow.

'On the bedside table there was a book, a book which has since disappeared, a book which you've held in your hand. And you declared that it was a play, I believe?'

'Yes.'

'Why did you say that?'

'Because it contained dialogues, nothing but dialogues.'

'Dialogues, nothing but dialogues... with the names of characters, I presume?'

'Yes, just as in every play, before each new line of dialogue. But I didn't remember the names, if that's your next question.'

'Did they sound classical?'

'I think so, but I couldn't be certain.'

'How many pages did you leaf through? One or two at the beginning, or more, going through the whole book? Think carefully before you answer, it's very important.'

Mrs. Johnson seemed more and more perplexed.

'Maybe a dozen, and not necessarily at the front of the book. Is it really so important?'

'More than you can imagine, madam. Do you remember the author of the book?'

'No, but I'm not even sure it was on the cover. I think there was only the title: *The King in Yellow*.'

'So what?' intervened the Scotland Yard inspector, even more perplexed than the witness. 'What's your conclusion, Burns?'

'That you did well to warn me, inspector. The situation is even worse than I thought. Because we now know that the *King in Yellow* which disappeared isn't the text of the official author—Robert W. Chambers, who wrote it fifteen years ago—but the play of the same name which relates to it. In the Chambers text there are only a few short excerpts from the play. It takes the form of a collection of short stories, centred around a play in two acts which is only quoted briefly, and whose peculiarity is that readers or spectators suddenly lose their reason from the second act on. They are seized by madness and commit suicide or kill each other. Or at least that's what Chambers claims in the short stories. For Mrs. Sanders to have chosen that for her bedtime reading is curious, to say the least. But to have the deadly play to hand, which, to my knowledge, has never been written, let alone printed... that would certainly explain her nightmare and the act of madness which followed.'

After a deathly silence, during which Alice was anxiously awaiting my friend's next words, he continued:

'The question now is whether reading the work was a voluntary act on her part, in which case where did she get hold of it and did she rashly do so to assuage her curiosity? Or did someone else put it there discreetly, in order for the unfortunate Victoria to read the noxious text before going to sleep?'

A short while later, Andrew Johnson had replaced his wife on the couch. He remembered the episode with the book, having been the one to notice it. He hadn't leafed through it, for he knew of the Chambers book and its reputation.

Fiddling with the gold watch chain across his waistcoat, he explained:

'I couldn't swear that the author's name was on the cover. I didn't pay much attention, as I had other things on my mind. I just knew it was the Chambers book, which is well known by amateurs of the genre. And citing the deadly play is a classic joke in the milieu of the theatre because everyone knows it doesn't exist.'

'If I understand correctly,' enquired Owen, 'you were an actor as well as a painter?'

'Yes,' replied Andrew with a nostalgic smile. 'Young and enthusiastic as I was at the time, I was confident of my talent. Alas, success never came. But everything changed when I met Victoria Sanders.'

After he'd gone over the circumstances again, Owen observed:

'You have many strings to your bow, sir, to say the least. I took a look at your painting in Mrs. Sanders' room. It's remarkable from every point of view. Miss Cheryl's grace is very well conveyed. Have you known her for a long time?'

'Yes, she was a model in the art school where I took classes. We got on well, and I enlisted her for a private session, with the result that you saw. I lost sight of her for several years after that. When I ran into her by chance a few months ago she was looking for work. I remembered I was in her debt and decided to hire her. Victoria didn't oppose it. That's the whole story.'

Despite his apparently frank explanation, his embarrassment was noticed by everyone. But Owen didn't insist. At least directly.

'I saw her in the company of your late boss's brother. They seemed to get on well together.'

'Cheryl is a very spontaneous girl,' he replied, and I noticed a vein throbbing on his temple. 'She's very natural, and not stand-offish at all. That individual decided to take advantage and vulgarly seduce her, as he did recently to my wife and doubtless countless other women before her. Daren is an unscrupulous thug, a notorious partygoer and gigolo, who would have bled his sister dry if she'd let him. Believe me, gentlemen, if there's anything fishy about her death, he'll be the one responsible.'

'Do you know the terms of Mrs. Sanders' will?'

'Not precisely. She led me to understand that I would take over the reins of the company if anything should happen to her. But clearly that parasite stands to inherit a packet. Despite his indiscretions and his regular visits to ask for money—she's not given in lately—and despite the fact she couldn't stand him any more, she's remained strangely attached to him. The only explanation must be family ties.'

Owen nodded his head, more in thought than in agreement. Then he observed:

'Your wife told us about her train accident. You were with her, I assume?'

'No, unfortunately,' sighed Andrew. 'I mean luckily, or I might not be here to answer your questions. She was very lucky in her misfortune, if you see what I mean. In fact, I think I was more affected than she was, for I heard the terrible news before learning that she was one of the survivors.'

'I can imagine your anxiety, sir.'

After that remark, in which I detected a tinge of irony, Owen questioned Johnson about the events of the night preceding the tragedy. He confirmed his wife's account. He'd been awakened by cries or moans at two o'clock in the morning, but hadn't felt like intervening. Why had he suggested getting his wife a glass of milk after she returned? Because she was in the habit of drinking one

69

before going to sleep. As was he. He'd asked Mrs. Benson to put a bottle and two glasses on a table in the corridor next to their room. That way, he hadn't needed to go down to the kitchen. As a consequence he couldn't say whether she was still there at half-past two. He'd woken up just after nine the next morning, to learn the tragic news shortly afterwards.

Asked whether he knew where *The King in Yellow* could be, he shook his head.

'Yellow is the colour of treason and cowardice,' he said, in a voice full of hate. 'The colour of tricksters and parasites. In your place, gentlemen, I wouldn't look too far. Your *The King in Yellow* may well be someone in this house, strutting around behind a mask, who hasn't fooled anyone for quite some time.'

After Wedekind had thanked Johnson, asking him not to leave the premises until further notice and to transmit the order to the others, Owen asked me, smilingly:

'So, Achilles, what do you think? Suspect or not?'

'I think the fellow has been truly shaken by the events, or he's an excellent actor. What about you?'

'Not only has he lost his boss, he's just lost his mistress and is furious. Our interview with Cheryl Chapman should clear things up. Meanwhile, I'd like to hear from our womaniser.'

10

CHEZ RITA

July 12, 1991

André, at the wheel of his car, observed that the scenery changed noticeably after Rennes, becoming starker. The mineral Celtic soil asserted itself and traces of civilisation dwindled, except for the presence of crosses. Crosses which always had a curious effect on him because, for some reason, they didn't appear particularly religious. Perhaps it was because they were so numerous they could practically serve as signposts. And because the ones he was used to seeing were massive, imposing, almost disquieting. At one point he'd just avoided seeing one from too close up, after he'd dozed off momentarily at the wheel and narrowly avoided a collision. That's when he'd allowed himself a brief rest after having driven for five hours without a break. He'd examined the cross, touched its rough grey surface and persuaded himself that there was a bond between them... but what? He'd shrugged his shoulders and attributed everything to fatigue. Or maybe it was a sign from above to be more prudent?

The clock on the dashboard showed two o'clock in the afternoon. It would be another hour before he arrived at Rita Messmer's residence. How had he located it so rapidly? Thanks to the marvellous **Célia**. **Her** lovely face seemed to appear before him as he cast his mind back to the moment two weeks ago, when he announced the absolute necessity of finding her.

Célia had been far from persuaded at the beginning:

'What good will it do us, darling?'

'According to Dr. Moreau, it's vital to my investigation.'

'To find your lost film?' she'd replied sceptically.

'And why not? Rita might remember.'

'You're joking. You'd be lucky if she even remembered you. You were only a child at the time.'

'Agreed. But if he thinks it's important, that must mean that he's taking things seriously, which is a good sign, is it not?'

'Well, in that case,' she'd said mockingly, 'I have no choice but to agree. It only remains to find this Rita.'

'That's to say find the needle in the haystack.'

'You don't need to tell me. But you're looking anxious, darling.'

'I am. You can believe me or not, but this investigation into the past is having a strange effect, as if I'd been personally involved in some past tragedy.'

'That's what your psychoanalyst thinks, isn't it?'

'He's not alone....'

'But that's their job! To flush out some mysterious Freudian memory from the past. And they always find one!'

Four days later, whilst André was still wondering how to go about the research, Célia burst into his study and placed a paper on his desk, on which the name Rita Messmer had been written, followed by an address in Brittany. André had looked at his wife in astonishment before stammering:

'How did you do it?'

'The simplest thing in the world. I hired a private detective. It wasn't free, but I'll put it on the household account. He told me that the mysterious Rita hasn't got a telephone and is away quite often, according to her neighbours, so it would be best to write for an appointment before going there.'

André had followed his wife's advice, and to his great surprise had received a letter from the woman in question a week later saying she would be delighted to see him the following Friday or Saturday.

And so it was that, one hour after touching the cross, he arrived in front of a small house, half hidden behind massive mauve hydrangea bushes. When he first saw the owner on the doorstep, after having rung the doorbell, he was filled with doubt. Certainly, with her hair wrapped in a scarf and her tinted spectacles, it was difficult to see her face. But how could this elderly woman with a nondescript figure, wearing an ill-becoming apron be the svelte and graceful Rita of his memories, with her cascade of black ringlets?

But Rita it was. And with a friendly smile she said she remembered him well, and invited him in.

A little later, in an overgrown garden, under an arbour invaded by clematis and a voluminous honeysuckle, they exchanged memories

72

over coffee and biscuits. Rita had a soft, rather weak voice, perhaps as a result of too many cigarettes, for she was a chain smoker.

She explained that she'd had a number of health problems, as a result of which she'd lost some of her hair, which is why she was never without a scarf. André replied that he'd always had a vivid recollection of her magnificent black hair, before proceeding to explain the reason for his visit.

As he'd anticipated, she had no recollection of the film which had made such a deep impression on him. She remembered that the Langlois—which was the real name of his friend Guy's parents, which he had transformed into "Lamblin" for Dr. Moreau—had a television set, for that was something of a rarity at the time. But to say whether it had broken down was too much to demand of her memory.

She pronounced this last phrase in a perfectly natural tone. Almost too natural to André's ears, and he started to doubt her sincerity. He preferred not to press the matter, however, opting to let his hostess lead the discussion.

'My brother and I had been friends with the Langlois for several years already. Heinrich had met Jean-Pierre—alias Jean-Paul—in a Berlin bar at the beginning of the fifties and they had painted the town red together. Heinrich had often spoken about him in glowing terms, so one day I accompanied him when he went to visit the Langlois. We got on well and saw each other frequently after that. Yes, I remember you... André, the inseparable friend of Guy. You got up to no good together, yet his little sister was so well-behaved. It's true she was only half your age. She was very pretty, but you rejected her disdainfully.'

'It's true. We weren't interested in girls yet.'

'And, regarding the year, I think it must have been 1966.'

'Are you sure?'

'Yes, because Jean-Pierre had lost his wife the year before in an accident.'

'I remember that as well. It made life very hard for them, although I don't think Guy fully understood at the time.'

'It's possible,' said Rita, shrugging her shoulders. 'I think he got on well with the housekeeper Jean-Pierre engaged afterwards. But not his young sister. So much so that she was obliged to limit the frequency of her visits. You remember that, no doubt?'

73

'Not really. I hardly paid any attention to her, to tell you the truth.'

'Of course,' said Rita, with an indulgent smile. 'You couldn't be expected to understand. Heinrich and I, on the other hand, visited Jean-Pierre regularly after the tragedy.'

Rita's weak voice grew even more faint and there was a faraway look in her eye. André pulled a face and declared:

'No, I didn't fully understand the situation. It had to have been a terrible blow for him, to suddenly find himself alone with two children. But he didn't show it.'

'Yes, at least not on the surface....'

'It was very considerate of you and your brother to comfort him so regularly.'

Rita, nodded, visibly moved.

'It was a tragedy,' she murmured, 'which affected all of us.'

'It's odd, but I don't recall seeing you or your brother after that.'

'Well... Heinrich left for Africa a year or two later, and I was sent to work in Bavaria.'

'And did you hear about Guy? He died at the age of fourteen in a car accident. His father was driving.'

Rita gave a deep sigh.

'Yes, but I didn't learn about it until later. How terrible! I saw Jean-Pierre one last time, in the mid-seventies. He'd managed to face the events with great courage. All he had left was his daughter, who had grown up. Several years later I learnt he'd died of cancer.'

After another silence, André observed:

'It's all very sad. But even after Guy's death, I didn't really appreciate what it would mean for me. I had other friends, and the sun was still shining. Nostalgia for old friends only seems to come over time.'

'Death is a concept which is difficult to grasp, even for adults.'

'Time goes by, and one forgets. For example, I can't remember the circumstances of Mme. Langlois's accident. What happened exactly? Did she drown?'

'No,' said Rita sombrely. 'She fell from the top of an old quarry. She was walking with her husband and some friends. She was standing apart from them, near the edge, when they heard her cry out. They rushed over but it was too late, of course. It was horrible. She'd fallen fifty feet and was lying there like a broken doll.'

'What a curious accident,' observed André thoughtfully. 'An adult falling alone, just like that.'

'What are you suggesting?' asked Rita sharply.

'Well, Mme. Langlois could have thrown herself off, for example. She was a very unhappy woman, I recall. Wasn't there an inquest?'

'Of course. But I don't really have any details. I was in Germany at the time. It's true that things dragged on a bit. But, as a dramatic playwright, you must be aware that the police are suspicious of everything. The suicide theory was abandoned after several witnesses said that, after the cry they saw the unfortunate woman struggling and trying to save herself, as if she'd just slipped.'

'I see. If she'd really wanted to end things, she would have been more discreet.'

'Suppose we talk about more pleasant things?'

André nodded his agreement. He couldn't decently have gone on. The conversation turned to the massive hydrangeas, and Rita explained that only the soil of Brittany could produce such magnificent specimens.

'As for my garden,' she said, looking around, 'it's gone to seed a bit because I haven't had the time to take care of it.'

'I think it's charming just the way it is.'

'So do the neighbourhood cats. As soon as the temperature drops, they come here. You can see for yourself if you've time to stay a little longer.'

'I'm afraid not. I have a long road ahead of me. You like animals, I take it?'

'Yes. They're all that's left to me.'

'I think I understand. You've lost loved ones yourself. A husband, perhaps?'

'No,' replied Rita, shaking her head. 'I never married. I... never mind. The past is the past. Let's leave it there, with all its cohorts of ghosts.'

'You're right,' agreed André, intrigued nonetheless by his hostess's gravity and the memory of her luxuriant black hair, now gone, which must have driven many of the men in her circle crazy.

'One last thing, madam, before I leave. I'd like to talk to your brother as well. Can you tell me where I can find him?'

Once more she shook her head dolefully.

75

'Heinrich has left us as well, I'm afraid. His remains must be somewhere in Africa, but no one knows where. His last letter, from Togo, was fifteen years ago.'

André decided to stop overnight at a hotel on the way back. His interview with Rita had left him perplexed, without knowing exactly why. All sorts of contradictory ideas filled his head, as well as a parade of ghosts and crosses. And the strange book left behind by a previous guest, which he devoured before falling asleep also contributed.

The next day, in the late morning, he was happy to see his wife, who greeted him with a broad smile. After he'd gone over his meeting with Rita she observed, thoughtfully:

'How bizarre, a brother disappearing without trace in Africa. Don't you think so?'

'Yes, but it's not just that. I don't understand why such a beautiful woman never married.'

'And do you think that means she led the life of a nun? How old-fashioned you are, darling.'

'Maybe, but things were different back then. And I got the distinct impression there's never been a man in her life, at least for quite a long time. Meanwhile, has anything been happening here?'

'Well, I haven't been idle, either,' said Célia. 'There's an envelope on your desk, with a photocopy inside. It's a newspaper article, but don't look at it just yet.'

'You intrigue me.'

'And Dr. Moreau dropped by last night.'

André stood petrified for a few moments, then blurted out:

'Don't tell me....'

'Yes. A new cassette. As he gave it to me, he wanted you to know that *The Unseen* was no longer invisible.'

11

DAREN

Narrative of Achilles Stock (continued)

'... My sister and I did not have a happy childhood, to put it mildly,' declared Daren Bellamy, with a distant smile. 'We were what is known as "false twins," born of the same mother, whom we never knew because she died giving birth on the twenty-fourth of April, 1876, in a dark street in Shoreditch. We were placed in the care of a family so impoverished that we were separated a few years later. The only memories I have are of dirt, hunger and screams from the fights of the two alcoholics in charge of our education—what a laugh! After that, I was entrusted to another family of the same ilk, whereas Victoria had better luck. She was even able to pursue studies worthy of the name. But, to be fair, she was more hard-working than I was. We lost sight of each other at around that time, and for quite a while. When we next saw each other, at seventeen or eighteen, and she became aware of the gap separating us, she did try to make me into a serious student without much success, despite the inevitable "think of your future" exhortations. It's true that she never stopped thinking along those lines, especially at the time that she was at least a little bit attractive, when she managed to marry her boss, old Sanders, who was twice as old as she was and who left her everything when he kicked the bucket. The Sanders inheritance was far from negligible, but do you think she would have the good taste to share the booty with her little brother? Not a chance. She continued to lecture me and didn't even offer me a cushy job in her company. She didn't trust me—who knows why? I was still young and hadn't yet realised that the female soul was unfathomable.'

'Too true,' agreed Owen, 'there's no greater mystery. And you are the living proof of the myth of equal opportunity. There are the penniless and the providers, the idiots and the brains; the dies of fate are cast from the beginning.'

Owen's comments, pronounced with great aplomb, could have been deemed to be offensive, but the amused and vaguely mocking smile never left Daren Bellamy's face. He might not have had such a blithe attitude had he read the telegram from the Yard which Wedekind had received shortly before he entered the room. The inspector, who had placed it in his pocket, was also smiling. I had thought, prior to the interview, that Owen would brandish his sharpest sword in his clash with the smug and odious Bellamy, but it was not to be. He adopted a measured, expectant attitude, and I even suspected him of submitting to the rascal's charm.

'And what happened, following all the blows fate dealt you? You seem to have resurfaced well enough.'

'I lived by expedient,' replied Daren, stroking his black hair, which he wore long. 'I did all kinds of jobs: waiter, bar pianist, encyclopaedia salesman, you name it.'

'Pianist?' echoed Owen.

'Whilst I was still young and idealistic, I was friends with a very gifted musician, who wanted to turn me into an accomplished pianist. She was more successful in the role of teacher than my sister. Though I must admit she had other arguments....'

Rubbing his neck with a retrospective smile, he added:

'So in that area I was a good student. I'm also pretty lucky with the horses and pretty good at cards.'

'There you are, the fairies didn't entirely neglect you at birth,' joked Owen. 'You have a few trumps in your hand.'

'You could say that,' replied Daren, lighting a cigarette.

'In any case,' interjected Wedekind, 'the fates probably haven't abandoned you from a financial point of view. It's unlikely your sister forgot you in her will.'

'The wheel turns. But I'm not counting my chickens.'

'Ah?' The policeman seemed surprised. 'Then you don't know the terms of her will?'

'Not really. She threatened to cut me out so many times I can't be sure of anything.'

'Well, we'll find out soon enough,' said the inspector. 'Anything else of note during your career to date? A major event, a notable success or failure?'

'No,' said Bellamy. 'At least nothing that stands out. If I were to go into detail about everything, we'd be here all night.'

Owen, who had been watching the man's hands, observed suddenly:

'That's quite a scar on your wrist.'

Holding out his arm to show it, Daren replied:

'As you can see, it isn't recent, if that's the drift of your remark.'

'The souvenir of a boxing match, or an over-passionate mistress?'

'That's my business,' replied Bellamy brusquely. 'All you need to know is that I can hold my own in a fight.'

'Noted,' retorted Wedekind in the same vein. 'Let's get back to the question of your alibi.'

'My alibi? What are you talking about, inspector? There's been no murder, as far as I know.'

'You know very well what I mean. Your sister's death remains suspicious, if only because of the size of her fortune. It's in your best interests to provide us with as much detail as possible about your movements at the time. You told us you'd left for town the previous evening, on the pretext of business, but in fact to party with your friends.'

'Play cards,' corrected Daren. 'Let's be accurate. And I've already provided you with a list of the friends in question, who are hardly the dregs of society.'

'The problem,' continued the policeman, 'is that there's a gap of five hours between the time the card game ended, at about one o'clock in the morning, and the time the receptionist saw you leaving your hotel, just after six.'

'During which time, naturally, I could have made a round trip here in a carriage and through heavily falling snow, in order to dispose of my sister by who-knows-what stratagem... maybe with a flying carpet?'

'In five hours such a lightning trip can't be ruled out.'

'So explain to me how Victoria could have been murdered. We found her in the middle of a field of virgin snow, except for her own footprints.'

'Precisely. It's the way it happened that I find curious. What a coincidence! You take a walk with Miss Cheryl, whom you've just met on the train, and you suddenly find yourself face-to-face with your sister's corpse.'

'I've explained to you a dozen times. Cheryl and I wanted some fresh air. Is that so surprising for two people cooped up in London most of the time?'

'And you just happen to come across the body.'

'We took the path to the cross, which is the only one in the area, and which Victoria herself took. Are people who make macabre discoveries automatically suspect? If so, people might stop reporting them and then you'd have to find them yourselves.'

Wedekind grumbled an indistinct remark to himself, then continued:

'You know, to kill someone you don't necessarily have to stand next to them with an axe. There are more subtle methods.'

'Such as?'

'Place a dangerously suggestive book on their bedside table.'

'Like that yellow book *The King in Yellow*? Seriously, inspector, don't tell me you believe in that nonsense. A book which can drive you mad, to the point of killing yourself. No such thing exists!'

'Nevertheless the book was on the table and had disappeared by the following morning... and, anyway, how do you know about it?'

'Because your men were looking for it and never stopped questioning us about it.'

'I'm talking about its harmful powers. Do you know the book?'

'Not personally, but Andrew told me about it. He's knowledgeable about literature.'

'And you aren't?' asked Owen.

'Not so much. I only read detective novels, Mr. Burns. It's the only literature I don't find annoying. I know that's not very intellectual.'

'On the contrary. All men of good taste read detective fiction.'

'Thank you for coming to my defence, Mr. Burns,' replied Daren with a smile of acknowledgement.

'And you're going to need it for what I have to tell you next,' said Wedekind sarcastically. 'I've just received a telegram from Scotland Yard about the Miller affair. Does that ring a bell?'

The news struck home. Daren Bellamy's smiling facade vanished, to be replaced by a picture of defeat. After a long silence, and with lips pursed, he replied:

'It had to happen, I knew it. Well, I must say, you haven't wasted any time, gentlemen.'

'That's not our habit at the Yard. And we have people with elephantine memories which can be triggered by key elements such as suspects' names. I don't have much information about the case for now, but it concerns a fifty-year-old widow, Jane Miller, who was savagely murdered by persons unknown ten years ago, and a young man bearing your name inherited her fortune. He was a prime suspect, but he turned out to have an alibi, so the case against him was dropped. You were the young man in question, were you not?'

'It's an old story,' sighed Daren.

'Ten years old, to be exact.'

'I was stony broke when I met Jane... One of those fortunate breaks I talked about earlier.'

'Let me guess; you, a twenty-five-year old lad, fell passionately in love with a woman twice your age.'

'No, not exactly. We were just good friends at the start. I was working for a second-hand dealer and had delivered a dresser she'd ordered. We hit it off; I told her about my problems and she told me about hers. She'd been desperately lonely since the death of her husband. How to describe it? We comforted each other mutually and saw each other regularly.'

'I understand,' said the policeman in a honeyed voice. 'What more noble than to help a damsel in distress! And, obviously, your bonds got tighter over time, to the point that she named you as her unique beneficiary. But, by a stroke of misfortune, she was murdered by an unknown assailant!'

Ignoring the sarcasm, Daren continued:

'That's right. It happened at dead of night, in a dark street, in driving rain. The investigation found that Jane had gone out to look for her dog, which had run away. But it also found I had an unshakeable alibi,' he added, looking defiantly at the inspector. 'I'd been at a party, in a well-known restaurant, with at least twenty witnesses present.'

'We'll come back to that, Mr. Bellamy,' declared Wedekind. 'And, believe me, all your alibis, recent and ancient, are going to be examined with a fine-tooth comb.'

Daren appeared to ignore the warning. He gave each of us an indecipherable look and declared solemnly:

'I'm fully aware of the opinion you have of me, gentlemen. I admit

I haven't always been a saint, but let me show you something.' He put his hand into the inside pocket of his velvet jacket. 'When I got my inheritance from Jane—which helped me out, but was far from astronomical—I also received a personal object which also became an exhibit. Before being attacked, Jane had lost her watch in front of her house. She never had the time to recover it however much she tried, which turned out to be fatal. We know this because there was a witness, by the way. Here's the object in question.'

He pulled a gold fob watch out of his pocket and placed it on the table.

'It was the last thing she saw before she died, like a link between life and death. Whenever I hold this watch, it's as if I'm in Jane's reassuring presence. And I'll never let go of it.'

12

THE UNSEEN

July 13, 1991

André had closed the shutters of the drawing room to provide sufficient darkness for the viewing. It was exactly half-past twelve and he had no thought of lunch. His usual tools when in creative mood were to hand: coffee and cigarettes. After taking a deep breath, he pressed the start button of the cassette player and sat back to watch. The usual white static appeared on the screen as the non-descript music started to swell. Soon the title appeared: *The Unseen,* followed by the names of the principal actors (Joel McCrea and Gail Russell) and the director (Lewis Allen). The music turned sinister and disquieting, as a street at night under driving rain occupied the screen. An old woman appeared and stopped after a few steps, intrigued by a house with lighted windows.

André shivered expectantly. The images he was watching matched his memories almost exactly. It was almost too good to be true! He pinched himself to prove he wasn't dreaming. Then a low-angle shot showed the woman, still under driving rain, in front of a line of sinister black railings. She bent down to pick up an object she'd just lost... A close-up revealed it to be a gold watch lying on the pavement streaming with rain.

André swallowed and tears came to his eyes. Only a couple of minutes had passed, and he was already convinced he was watching the long-lost film. The gold watch alone, in such a sinister setting, had swept away any remaining doubts... Suddenly a prowling figure chased the old woman through an alleyway, with suggestive shadow-play, followed by a close-up of her terrified face, before she fell down under the blows of her aggressor. It was the same terrified face which had haunted him over the years. When he saw the face of a young boy with his face pressed against a window, a partial witness to the incident, he seemed to recognise that scene as well. What followed was more banal, with a widower engaging a pretty young woman—with whom he would gradually fall in love—to look after his children. The scene with the door knob, which he awaited anxiously, eventually appeared. And in two parts, exactly as he remembered. One scene of the knob turning slowly, and a terrified young woman with her back to the door, her pretty face glistening with perspiration; and a second of the brass lock, as if the dangerous murderer roaming the neighbourhood wanted to force his way in. The revelation of the guilty party would have come as no surprise to anyone accustomed to the genre of film, exactly as he recalled. The closing scene featuring the white spiral staircase banished any remaining doubts he might have had.

André remained for a few moments in the armchair, as if paralysed by the intense emotional shock. A dream he'd had for twenty years had just come true. The impossible had happened, thanks to his perseverance and that of Dr. Moreau, to whom he owed a huge debt of gratitude. Célia, who had doubtless noticed the silence at the end of the film, stuck her head round the door. Smiling broadly, she asked:

'Well, was that it?'

'Yes, darling, there's no doubt about it. You can laugh if you like, but I'm still in a state of shock. Be good, serve me a Scotch.'

'I knew already,' she said mischievously.

'Ah? Did you watch it before me?'

'No, I wouldn't have dared! Take a look in the envelope and you'll understand. Stay there and I'll get you your whisky.'

After André had swallowed half the glass, he took the piece of folded paper out of the envelope. It was a photocopy of a newspaper article, as Célia had said, giving details of the France 2 television channel for September 23rd, 1966. *The Unseen,* by Lewis Allen, had been broadcast at eight o'clock.

'I didn't want to spoil your pleasure,' she explained, 'or influence the delicate machinery of your memory, darling. And you were right, it was autumn 1966 and you were exactly ten years old at the time.'

'You've done a remarkable job, darling. I don't know how to thank you.'

'You know very well,' she replied, sitting in his lap, placing her hands on his neck and looking him in the eye:

'You've realised your dream, but I haven't yet realised *mine*.'

'I'm entirely at your disposal.'

'Don't play the idiot! You know exactly what I mean.'

'Yes, of course,' he sighed. 'But I have to confess that things aren't as simple as that.'

Célia stiffened:

'What do you mean?'

'I'm wondering if Dr. Moreau isn't right. My obsession about this film is excessive. When I look at it, it affects the very core of my being, as if there's something else deep down inside me.'

'So you need another consultation.'

'Of course, if only to thank him. You must admit, he's done a remarkable job.'

'It's true, you owe him a lot. As for me, I would be more nuanced.'

'I confess, I'm nervous about a new session.'

'But André, get a grip on yourself. You can't go back now.'

'I know, but I feel so strange these days. For example, on the drive up to Brittany, the simple view of a cross had a strange effect on me, as if I were a captive in the middle of a spider's web, with the monstrous creature waiting for me.'

'And did this spider have a face, by any chance?'

'No, it's more a symbol... of Fate, which perfidiously spins the web of life.'

'You seem to be seeing a lot of symbols lately.'

'True, but our world, modern though it may be, is still a jungle, where everyone is a predator.'

'You need to stop spinning webs yourself, my dear. Your profession as a dramatic author is starting to play you tricks.'

'And don't you spin webs all day in front of the mirror, my dear, perfecting creations to seduce the opposite sex.'

'So, then, why don't we combine our efforts.'

So saying, she left the room and returned shortly with a well-thumbed notebook. Finding the page she wanted, she placed it under her husband's nose.

André, who knew the text by heart, nodded silently.

After a moment, Célia declared:

'We should eat. My stomach is crying out from hunger. Get up! You're not going to spend the whole day in that armchair.'

So saying, she placed a tender kiss on her husband's cheek.

André still didn't feel reassured. A biblical image had come to mind, that of Lot's wife as she fled Sodom. Despite being warned, she turned to look behind her before being touched by the finger of God.

Looking back and delving into the past could have deadly consequences.

13

CHANDRA AND CHERYL

Narrative of Achilles Stock (continued)

Chandra Ganesh was a handsome man, with a noble presence. He was wearing silk attire of a bright violet colour which went well with his swarthy complexion, black beard and eyes which shone like sapphires. His youthful bearing contrasted with the wise expression on his face. In fact, he'd been born in a Chhipa community in Jodhpur, India in 1860 and had met Mrs. Sanders when she was on a business trip there. She'd been very impressed with his professional abilities as a dyer and had invited him to come to England and work for her.

'And you followed her just like that?' asked Owen with a friendly smile.

'It was written. I've never had cause to regret her confidence in me, nor mine in her.'

'You more or less abandoned your previous profession, to enter into service with her.'

'The past can never be abandoned, sir, and she never treated me as a servant in the Western sense of the word.'

'Dyer,' said Owen thoughtfully, 'a great and noble profession, rare here. Working with indigos and madders to create beautiful tints, what a pleasure! Please don't think I'm trying to flatter you. As my friend Achilles here can attest, I've always held that beauty resides in form and colour.'

'That's true for the beauty of appearances,' agreed Chandra. 'But there exist other forms of beauty, Mr. Burns, if I may be so bold.'

'So those potted plants I noticed in the greenhouse belong to you, I assume? I say that because I couldn't identify them and only a few species can survive in such temperatures.'

A pale smile appeared on the Hindu's solemn face.

'You're very observant. I'm not surprised, for I am aware of your reputation and the debt that officers of the law owe to you. If I'm ignorant of the secrets of your talent, perhaps you will allow me to guard mine.'

'Of course,' said Owen, smiling reflexively, but disconcerted by the other's diplomacy. 'To each his art. That said, mine has not yet allowed me to unravel the mystery surrounding Mrs. Sanders' death. Perhaps you have an idea of what might have happened? I imagine the suicide theory seems unlikely to you. She wasn't that kind of woman, was she?'

Chandra Ganesh looked into the distance.

'You're right. Ending one's life is not common in my family, and I considered Mrs. Sanders to be my sister. As for the rest, I can only say she went to her destiny. Only she knows what happened and why. The stars which witnessed the event will reveal the truth somehow, one day.'

Alarmed by the turn the interview was taking, Wedekind intervened to set it on more prosaic lines. Despite his precise replies, Chandra was unable to shine any new light on the other testimonies, which he confirmed in their details. He was sleeping the sleep of the just at the time of death. He'd noticed the yellow book on the bedside table the night before, but he'd never seen it there earlier. He didn't read much fictional literature. As for his views on the victim's brother, he replied that his role was not to judge. In his view, aberrant behaviour often concealed personal malaise. His mistress had asked him to be indulgent on her brother's behalf, and that's what he'd tried to do.

When Wedekind thanked him, Chandra bowed respectfully before taking his leave. Owen told him with calm assurance:

'The light of truth will eventually shine, Chandra. Do not worry.'

'It's shining already, sir, I've seen it.'

After the tall, violet-clad figure had gone, I turned to Owen:

'What on earth did he mean by that?'

'If only I knew, Achilles,' replied Owen, equally perplexed. 'If only I knew.'

'Come, gentlemen,' cautioned Wedekind, 'don't be fooled by his visionary fakir routine. I know the type, I've dealt with dozens of them already. They give themselves great airs, but there's nothing there. I'm going to call the last witness. I warrant that the mere sight of her will bring colour to your cheeks, gentlemen!'

On the last point at least, Wedekind was right. Owen recovered his verve the instant that the ravishing Cheryl Chapman stepped into the room. He seized control of the interview, dismissing any vague attempts by the inspector to intervene. The dialogue which followed scarcely conformed to the norms of a police investigation. The subject of her previous activities as a model seemed to dominate all other considerations, which didn't seem to bother Miss Cheryl at all.

'It's not as easy as you might think, Mr. Burns,' she explained, adjusting her pink bolero. 'It demands a lot of patience and impeccable physical form.'

'I imagine so, miss. But it's obvious that you have what it takes.'

'So I've been told, and I've ended up believing it,' she replied, trying to look demure, and succeeding. 'It also requires a lot of training and sacrifice, for one always has to resist temptation and avoid sweet things.'

'Speaking personally, I can resist everything but temptation. But what do you mean by "a lot of training"?'

'Exercises to improve suppleness, practising poses in front of a mirror.'

'Practices that you haven't lost, I presume?'

'Not at all. I still pose for designers today. But Andrew's not happy about it. He says it doesn't go with my secretarial activities. He's become quite old-fashioned these last few years. In that sense he's changed. And, anyway, who knows what will happen tomorrow? This tragedy is proof of that. I don't know as of today what my future is with the Sanders company.'

'If I understand correctly, your relations with Mr. Johnson are good, insofar as you knew him previously?'

'Of course. I do my best never to let him down. From a professional point of view, I mean.'

'And for the rest?' asked Owen in a deceptively casual manner.

'Well,' she hesitated, 'it's a bit tricky. We were close at one time. But now it's no longer the same. First of all, there's his wife, who has a dim view of me. And he himself has become very serious. He doesn't like it that I'm playing around with Daren.'

'Whom you met in the train coming down?'

As she explained the circumstances, I became convinced that the deceased's brother didn't only have enemies in the house. Cheryl explained herself with a fervour that betrayed her sentiments. The episode of the cross, for example, where she heard him complain behind her back, was described with a fair degree of hilarity. It was obvious that Daren Bellamy had made a new conquest. But for now Miss Cheryl was practically penniless, so one could hardly suspect him of dowry-chasing—although the supple and generous curves of this ravishing blonde were reason enough to attract the interest of our principal suspect.

Regarding her activities on the night of the tragedy, she had been alone in her London flat and had gone to bed late after packing her bags. As no one could confirm or deny it, Owen turned his attention to her relations with her mistress.

'What did I think of Mrs. Sanders? She was a straight arrow. She'd been a little suspicious at first, but she quickly changed her opinion. I gave the job my best so as not to disappoint her. She also understood that I was the "Eve in Orient" that she appreciated so much. She was not a pitiless businesswoman. And she had good judgment. The only time she was wrong was on the subject of her brother. I can tell you, he's not the man she thought he was.'

'Have you any idea what could have happened to your mistress?'

With a thoughtful pout, she replied:

'Yes and no. I don't know what was in her head when she went out for that nocturnal walk, but as for the rest, she stumbled and had the misfortune to strike her head against that stone. I can't see any other explanation. Nobody could have approached her, there were only her footprints in the snow.'

After we had thanked her, Wedekind observed:

'A little naive, but full of good sense, that girl. And I'm beginning to wonder if she's not right about what happened. Nothing but a winged creature could have approached Mrs. Sanders to strike a fatal blow. And I find it very hard to believe that a simple book can push a person to suicide, particularly since her behaviour doesn't bear that out.'

'In other words, we've been barking up the wrong tree and Daren Bellamy is perfectly innocent?'

Inspector Wedekind clenched his fists:

'He doesn't give that impression, I admit, but the facts are there: nobody, absolutely nobody could have committed such a murder!'

14

THE OLD QUARRY

July 16, 1991

'I felt sure it was the right picture this time!' announced Dr. Moreau with a satisfied smile, leaning back in his armchair with his hands over his ample stomach. 'I was even certain of it. And I couldn't resist taking a peek before I gave it to your wife. The gold watch on the pavement: as soon as I saw that, I knew we'd won!'

'All credit to you, Doctor,' said André. 'You can't imagine how grateful I am.'

The psychoanalyst modestly ignored the remark. He placed his fingertips under his chin, closed his eyes, and continued:

'I must admit I was slightly mistaken about the clue of the gold watch. It had to be taken at face value as one of the key images of the film. But that doesn't mean that any idea of a parallel link must be ruled out. We have to stay vigilant. I recommend to see the film again, calmly, and be very attentive to detail.'

'I've already done so, several times. To the point that my wife threatens to make it disappear, if she surprises me watching it again.'

'It could bring us new information. I say "could" because our investigation has now taken another direction. And not the one I'd assumed at the start, namely a personal and disquieting souvenir buried in the very depths of your memory, not to say a more mysterious phenomenon, resembling a form of reincarnation. There, also, I was wrong. Everything points, from now on, to a genuine criminal affair whose gravity you subconsciously realised. I tell you frankly that's the only way to explain the reaction of that Rita, frightened by the mere view of a detective film. And claiming not to remember it when you asked her about it.'

'I only spoke to her about the film, not her reaction to it,' clarified André. 'That would have been too delicate. She didn't create a bad

91

impression. On the contrary, she was charming.'

'Surely you don't believe she would have confessed straight away to a crime in which she was involved?'

'Of course not. I merely said she didn't strike me as someone capable of such an act. That said, I did notice that she became nervous when I started to probe what happened to Mme. Lamblin. She quickly changed the subject.'

'There you are,' said the psychoanalyst, nodding his head eloquently.

'So, according to you, that accident wasn't really....'

'Probably not, and I might add that the motive is pretty obvious... André, don't tell me you haven't worked it out. The account of your meeting with this person makes it glaringly obvious.'

'A crime of passion?'

'Obviously! You yourself, when you were only ten years old, had a vivid memory of a woman as beautiful as Snow White, with red lips and long black locks. Someone like that couldn't help but dazzle the men around her.'

'In other words, Jean-Pierre Lamblin.'

'Of course. Think about it. Think of the frequent visits Rita made to his home.'

'She was always accompanied by her brother,' objected André.

'What difference does that make? He was simply her alibi. She couldn't very well go there regularly by herself. It's obvious she had a relationship with the father of your friend Guy.'

'I didn't notice anything out of the ordinary.'

'You were only ten years old. How could you understand anything like that?'

'That's true,' admitted André. 'So, according to you, they were lovers who decided to get rid of the superfluous spouse by arranging an accident.'

'Yes, it's the most obvious explanation, based on the facts at our disposal.'

'So why didn't they marry afterwards? And why did Rita stop coming after a while?'

'That I can't say, although it could be something as simple as a break-up. As Pascal says, "the heart has its reasons, of which reason knows nothing". Perhaps you could go over the part of your interview which covered Mme. Lamblin's accident, trying not to omit any detail.'

After listening attentively to his visitor, Dr. Moreau observed:

'Hmm. The fact that Rita claimed to have been in Germany at the time, giving her a cast-iron alibi, is suspect, to say the least.'

'But in that case she couldn't have killed Mme. Lamblin.'

'Of course—although we've only her word for it. In any case, it could have been her lover who carried out the base deed.'

'He was some distance from his wife when she fell into the void. And no one, apparently, could have approached her without being seen.'

The psychoanalyst shrugged his shoulders:

'At this stage we can only speculate, but we can't depend on the testimony of Rita Messmer alone. The best thing would be for you to visit her a second time and question her in the light of our new deductions. Discreetly, of course, to be on the lookout for her reactions when you address the sensitive points. That is, if you're serious about pursuing your investigation....'

'As a matter of fact,' said the young playwright hesitantly, 'I'm no longer so sure. For me, the essential has been accomplished.'

'You've found the cult film of your childhood.'

'Yes, thanks to you. And it's given me a boost, like finding the sacred flame! What's more, I've started work again. I've had a great idea, which I've already committed to paper.'

'Excellent news, André! I'm happy for you. But permit me to insist, try to see Rita again, if only to get a clearer idea. Otherwise, this uncertainty may come back to haunt you, with the consequences you know about already.'

'Very well. But I shall wait for a few days before contacting her.'

'And, as a practical matter, you could do some research on newspaper reports of the event. You've enough information to start. Where did it happen, by the way?'

Slumped in the armchair, André ran his hands through his hair, before replying:

'I prefer to be vague about it. It's not only about me, but another person who....'

'I understand,' replied Dr. Moreau. 'We'll leave the matter there. Don't be embarrassed. Several of my patients feel the same way.

Never mind about the coast where Mme. Lamblin fell to her death.'

'Coast?' repeated André in astonishment. 'Why "coast"? Did I say anything of the sort?'

'No, but you spoke of a cliff, and I thought of the sea.'

'Maybe because of my trip to Brittany. I understand. I didn't explain very well, it was an old quarry.'

There was a deep silence, broken eventually by the psychoanalyst.

'An old quarry, you say?'

'Yes. I suppose there was a cliff there.'

'I understand,' replied the other testily. 'But why didn't you tell me that before?'

'Is it important?'

'Maybe not,' replied Dr. Moreau. 'Maybe it's just a coincidence, a simple coincidence....'

15

THE STARS

January 10, 1911

In the cold late-afternoon, the oblique rays of the sun caressed the red bricks of Raven Lodge, the immaculate white of the snow and the speckled darkness of the surrounding woods. But it was like a match about to be extinguished. The bluish shadows of the night lay in wait, ready to regain their territory in a few hours. Some marauding crows were dispersing at the point where the carriage bearing the detectives was receding. They had come to notify the inhabitants of the terms of Victoria Sanders' last will and testament. Standing at one of the drawing room windows, Andrew Johnson watched the vehicle disappear into the distance. When he turned round, he saw that only Alice was still present. Chandra, Cheryl and Daren had left. That was probably for the best, he told himself, his face flushed.

'I didn't know she'd sold so much of the company to stockholders.'

'What difference does it make for you, Andrew?' asked his wife, installing herself on the sofa and picking up her knitting. 'She pretty well left you in charge of the company, isn't that what counts?'

'A mere director, at the whim of the stockholders. What a gift! It was the very least she could do.'

'You're exaggerating, Andrew. There are many in the company who'll envy you.'

'And what difference does that make?' he continued, clenching his fists. 'The sale increased her personal fortune considerably. A fortune which has just passed into the hands of that thug, her brother. You heard how much that represents. He has enough to last him the rest of his life, despite his outrageous spending habits.'

'I'm just as pleased as you are.'

'It's repugnant!'

'I've always told you he was repugnant, but you wouldn't listen.'

'It's true! I should have thrown him out with my own hands, the second he stuck his nose in.'

'But it's a family affair, Andrew. It was the deceased's wish, there's nothing we can do.'

'A family affair, that's what I believe as well. If I'd chased her brother away, maybe Victoria would still be alive.'

'You wouldn't have had the courage or the physical force. You have nothing to regret. What surprises me is the amount she left to that little hussy, almost the equivalent of two years' salary. That was really generous on her part.'

'Let me remind you that Chandra got even more.'

'And do you find that unfair? Weren't they very close? Really, Andrew, I have the impression you systematically defend that little tease. And I have to wonder why, because she doesn't return the favour. Not these days, anyway!'

'Shut up, if you please,' said Andrew, now crimson.

'But, after all, maybe she made the right choice. Unpleasant though he may be, our ugly duckling Daren has just changed into the golden goose!'

Feeling the blood beginning to boil in his veins, Andrew took leave of his wife, slamming the door furiously behind him.

Alice shook her head with a smile of commiseration, then, unable to concentrate, put her knitting down. She stood up and went out into the corridor, from whence the imposing white staircase led to the upstairs rooms. Cheryl and Daren were probably up there. Staring at the flight of stairs, she decided that was not the right direction. She recalled that the policeman had asked them to stay in the house at least one more day, which had made Andrew even angrier. She walked along the corridor as far as the kitchen, where she found only Mrs. Benson working in front of the oven. She went through the adjacent laundry, which gave access to the greenhouse, where she found Chandra tending to the potted plants.

They said nothing to each other for a long moment, before she asked him what he was doing.

'I'm continuing my dyeing work,' he replied in his calm voice.

'To keep your hand in?'

'If you like... in fact I never lost it. Painting the world with colour is my mission.'

There followed a discussion on the theme of colour, which Chandra developed with much erudition. In his native country, it had considerable symbolic importance. Each colour was associated with sentiments and events and some of his compatriots chose to wear different clothes each day, consistent with such considerations.

'That's fascinating,' said Alice, watching him grind the small flowers from his pots in a mortar and pestle. 'But what are those? I've never seen such flowers.'

'Very few people know of them, even in India.'

'They scarcely have any colour.'

'They're colourless. At least for most mortals. In fact, they produce the most beautiful colour in the universe. A unique colour, totally different from all others. But only for those who can see. It's only accessible to certain rare initiates. Otherwise it's totally invisible.'

'So I shall never see it.'

'It's very unlikely, madam. You would have to follow a special treatment, which I cannot divulge. It's my mission to produce such a colour.'

Alice frowned:

'But if it's invisible, what purpose does it serve?'

Chandra smiled indulgently, then fixed the young woman with his sapphire gaze.

'Since I've been here in Raven Lodge, I've spread its perfume everywhere. That's why I brought the pots. That will allow... But come back to see me later, after dinner, when it will be darker. You will better understand my role.'

'I'll do my best,' stammered Alice, who sensed the Indian's hypnotic gaze penetrate to the very core of her being.

'Meanwhile, let me give you something.'

So saying, he reached up to one of the shelves, brought down a small flacon, and handed it to her.

'Guard it carefully, it could be useful one day.'

'What is it?' asked Alice in astonishment. She could only see a thick milky liquid in the small glass container.

'A paste I've made from alum, crushed bone, and the urine of a particular species of cow. It's remarkably effective and can join together the most tenuous surfaces. Also, it's almost invisible. It can't be seen once it's been used, even by breaking the assembled parts.'

'I don't understand at all,' she replied, holding the flacon with her fingertips, as if it were a stick of dynamite. 'What has this got to do with what's happened? With the cursed book, or whatever?'

'It has nothing to do with such trivialities, I can assure you. You will realise its usefulness at the right time, when a new life is offered to you.'

Standing in front of the dresser mirror in her room, Cheryl examined her *contrapposto* with a critical eye. She had thrown logs in the small hearth before beginning her daily routine, and the flames added a copper glow to her milky skin. With satisfaction, she noted that her figure was as firm and supple as ever. How much longer could Daren resist her charms? Only a few days; she knew what men were like. But she'd better get to work as well, for it wouldn't do for him to start looking elsewhere. After donning a cream-coloured close-fitting silk gown, she went down to the drawing room. She suppressed a grimace on finding Andrew alone there, glass in hand.

With a strange mixture of admiration and controlled anger, he told her she was beautiful. Without a word, she went to the drinks table and served herself a whisky. Andrew came over to her.

'What game are you playing?' he asked, his breath reeking of alcohol.

'Whatever game I want, Andrew. You're not my father.'

'That's it, I don't mean anything to you any more,' he said through clenched teeth.

'Take your hand off my shoulder, please.'

'You seem to have forgotten all that I've done for you.'

'Isn't it really the reverse? How many times have you told me that you owed me everything, that my beauty had sublimated your talent, to the point of changing your life?'

'Maybe so. But I have trouble believing that you could forget everything, just like that, for a thug who will discard you after a couple of weeks.'

A sharp noise echoed in the room as Andrew rubbed his cheek, bright red from the slap he'd just received.

'So sorry. I couldn't help myself. But you asked for it.'

His senses dulled by the alcohol, Andrew drew himself up to his full height and grabbed her roughly by the arm.

'How could—.'

But he got no further. Daren, full of smiles, had just come into the room.

'Hmm. Looks as though I came at the wrong time. Or the right one, depending on your point of view. Andrew, would you mind letting go of the lady. Don't make Prince Charming come to her aid. Cheryl, you're even more adorable than usual in that gown. Don't pull that face Andrew. We'll be dining shortly and you need to recover your posture as the perfect gentleman. You're head of the company, that counts for something, surely? What would your dear Alice say if she were to see you like that, drunk with jealousy or jealously drunk? It wouldn't do. Be a good fellow and serve me a drink, so we can toast our reconciliation.'

It was almost ten o'clock when Alice left her dinner companions, without the slightest regret. Dinner had been served late, by a Mrs. Benson who declared that it might be her last, seeing as how, from now on, she had no commitment to anyone present. Nobody had spoken loudly during the meal, but there had been plenty of whispered allusions. Her husband hadn't touched the wine, which was a good thing because he certainly hadn't skimped on the aperitif. Chandra, who had tried to keep things calm, was the first to leave the table. Cheryl, Daren and Andrew had stayed behind. Maybe they'd wanted to talk privately, she thought with amusement.

When she reached the greenhouse, she was greeted by a glacial blast and was thankful she'd brought a heavy shawl along. The glass door leading to the outside was wide open. From the doorway she could see Chandra motionless in the snow, looking up at the heavens filled with stars. She went to join him, taking his arm, in the belief that the intense cold authorised such a move. She had thought about his strange words, but to no avail. If it had been anyone else, she would have dismissed the words as meaningless gibberish. But the Indian had so much wisdom and his comportment was so calm, that all doubt vanished.

'Can you see the magnificent sky?'

'I can.'

'What does it inspire in you?'

'The sense of the infinite, the unknown, and the realisation of our insignificance here below.'

'That's the constellation of Orion, known to the Ancients. It's easily recognisable by the alignment of three stars, known as the Three Magi, here in the west.'

'They're magnificent.'

'There are other constellations with the names of the heroes of Antiquity, immortalised in the firmament. Andromeda, Perseus and many others.'

'Their history is written in the stars,' said Alice dreamily.

'So true. But I have the impression your remark is based on a precise, personal reason.'

'It's true. I had the opportunity to verify it for myself.'

'Then you know it's not just a poetic image. In truth, *all* stories are written in the stars. The stars know everything. Look up there. The thousand eyes of the night are observing us. They're always watching.'

Alice shivered. She believed everything her companion was saying. Then she asked:

'And does that have something to do with your invisible colour?'

'Yes. Because that colour gives to the things surrounding it a light which can be seen from very far away.'

'For those who know how to see it,' murmured Alice, who, fascinated, scanned the sky encrusted with diamonds.

'Yes, you've understood, I believe. But it is not within my power to tell you more.'

After leaving the Indian, Alice returned to the central corridor. The magic of those strange moments had overwhelmed her. She felt herself invaded by the glacial cold of reality. She tried to look at things objectively. Chandra was neither a madman, nor a clairvoyant. It was his religion which instilled his strange beliefs. She reached her room, where her husband was noticeable by his absence. She didn't care where she was. She slipped quickly under the covers where, eyes wide open in the darkness, she could still see the myriad stars sparkling.

At midnight, amidst the wide snowy expanse, Raven Lodge appeared to be asleep. But Chandra, since the death of Mrs. Sanders, had become a light sleeper. His remorse at not having been able to protect her gnawed at him. His ears remained attuned to the deep silence.

Suddenly, he sat bolt upright. Someone was up. He detected a faint purring noise, but unlike someone asleep. Flames in the chimney? On the ground floor? The noise faded, but he preferred to be sure. A few moments later, he descended the stairs stealthily, but the steps creaked feebly under his weight. In the corridor he noticed a light from the open door of the drawing room. He advanced slowly and peeked inside.

The room was empty, but there was a fire in the grate. He went to look. The fire was almost out: there was only a small piece of cardboard burning... and it was yellow. He made the instant connection with the missing book and quickly pulled it from the flames. But it burnt his fingers, so he threw it in the air and collected what was left after extinguishing the remaining flames under his shoe.

He took stock of the situation. This book-burning was obviously very recent. Its instigator could not be far—even hiding in the room, if he'd heard Chandra coming. He looked slowly around. Nothing obvious, but the light in the hearth was going out, and conditions were not ideal. He moved forward slowly, passed by a curtain without examining it, and didn't see the hand which emerged to pick up a heavy ashtray from a nearby table.

Acting on a hunch, Chandra turned suddenly. But he only had time to recognise a familiar face, reddened by the light of the embers and with strangely brilliant eyes, before a painful blow resonated in his skull.

16

THE NEBULAE

July 18, 1991

André arrived late at Carl Jelenski's mill that evening. He'd dropped by that morning and the astronomer had suggested he come back later in order to benefit from a pure sky, to contemplate the stars.

For the rest of the day, André had worked non-stop on his latest play with astonishing ease. This time, the work was not exclusively a detective story. He'd injected a considerable dose of the fantastic, using the power of words in a way he'd never done before. Maybe he'd gone too far—it was almost provocative, to the point he wondered if he'd find a taker. It didn't matter. He felt he had to write it; that he was in the process of writing a masterpiece. That was all that mattered. The idea had come to him that evening, on the way back from Brittany, when he'd read parts of the book which had been left in his hotel room. It was a collection of stories by a certain Robert W. Chambers. The title of the book had caught his eye. He would use it for his new play. He had to!

He'd written the last word at a quarter past ten—he was in the habit of recording the time he finished the first draft of a new work. Obviously, the text would require a number of revisions. But the essence was there, on paper, just as if it were engraved in marble. In four days, a record for him, even if it was relatively short: two acts. He knew better than anyone that it wasn't length that gave a play quality. Afterwards, he'd put the pages in a folder, which he'd placed in a drawer under some other papers. He didn't want Célia to look at it out of curiosity....

It was after eleven when Carl Jelenski took him to the top of the mill, to his famous observatory. After climbing a steep wooden staircase they reached the top level, dimly lit by a red light—which didn't affect visual acuity, the astronomer explained. A voluminous telescope encircled with brass gleamed in the centre of the room, which was also tightly stacked with maps, other instruments, and books on the subject. The air was almost suffocating.

'On the menu tonight we have two nebulae,' said Carl, eyes gleaming mischievously behind thick lenses. 'Two choice pieces, amongst the most beautiful and the most visible. And we're in luck with the weather.'

He adjusted the telescope and invited André to take a look. To his stupefaction, he saw a vast luminous expanse dotted with a remarkable group of stars.

'The Lagoon nebula,' commented the astronomer. 'And a bit higher, to the right, you can see Trifid, which is slightly smaller. They're both about four thousand light-years away. In other words, what you're seeing corresponds to a very distant past.'

'Four thousand years,' repeated André, fascinated. 'It's incredible.'

'And for the galaxies, you have to multiply by a thousand. Two million light-years for Andromeda, the nearest one to our earth.'

'Where are Hyades and Aldebaran?'

'In the Taurus constellation. You can't see it yet, you have to wait until late autumn. Why do you ask?'

'Because that's where the mysterious city of Carcosa is located. I talk about it in the play I'm writing. It's lit by two suns, and when the moon rises, you can see it shine between the distant towers of the city. Don't try to understand, it's pure fiction.'

'I see you've recovered your imagination, my boy. It's good that you finally found your film.'

'I feel like another man, but one who feels very small in the universe. This gigantic clockwork mechanism, I believe you called it. And what would happen if it stopped?'

'Nothing good for us, believe me.'

'And what if it started turning in the opposite direction? Could we go back in time?'

'In theory, yes,' chuckled the professor, 'but there may be a few practical problems.'

'One could kill one's parents, so they couldn't give birth to us.'

'A typical idea from an author. But even if we can't go back to the past, we can at least see it.'

104

'As I am at the moment. There: I can see Trifid. Very beautiful, too.'

'I wasn't thinking so much about the stars, but about sequences of life here on earth.'

'I'd like to believe you,' replied André cautiously.

'It's easy to understand, or at least the basic principles are. But before that, imagine a celestial object, not a star but more like a planet, surrounded by a special kind of gas whose consistency could be modified. A gas so dense that its surface shines like a mirror. Now imagine that we can modify its density gradually in places, so that the surface, depending on the point of view chosen, appears flat not spherical. Suppose further that it could be bent, so it behaves like the magnifying mirror of the telescope you're looking through now. Do you follow me?'

'Perfectly. It's as if we placed giant magnifying mirror on the moon, for example, pointing at the earthly observer. He would see his own reflection with a delay of—.'

'One or two seconds,' replied Jelenski. 'Which is negligible, of course. But with a celestial object situated fifty light-years away, you could see what happened at that spot a hundred years ago.'

Abandoning his observation, André turned towards his host, whom he could see only dimly in the darkness.

'You're giving me ideas, professor. I could use them for my next project. And I admit the reasoning is valid, from a theoretical point of view.'

'Good! Then all you need now is to lose your preconceived ideas, confined to a miserable binary logic. Suppose we pursued this line of thought over a glass or two?'

After two whiskies, André was indeed more receptive, helped no doubt by the atmosphere of the astronomer's den.

'Compare a robot and a man. A crude, rigid technology on the one hand and the miracle of the human body on the other. It's the difference between our knowledge and that of superior spirits; the difference between the creator of the classic mirror and that of the gaseous, modifiable type I've just described.'

'That's all very well, but how to conceive of a light signal which can propagate itself with such precision over such great distances?'

'It's the principle I spoke to you about last time. Imagine a colour unknown to the solar spectrum, of unimaginable beauty, and the power not to encounter an obstacle in its sphere of influence.'

'Yes, I remember. But you also told me it would be invisible to most mortals.'

'True. And that's where those famous plants described in my late archaeologist friend's manuscript come in.'

'By absorbing them one could see that unimaginably beautiful colour?'

'It's not as simple as that,' replied Jelenski, still with his affable smile, 'but let's just assume so. The biggest problem is that the colour must be spread throughout a given zone to be effective. It's a sort of perfume derived from plants. A delicate operation which can only be revealed to certain initiates.'

'In other words, only certain chosen spots in the past could become visible?'

'Correct, without talking about problems of astral conjunction, which could limit the visions to precise moments during the year. You understand that the gaseous "mirrors" must be positioned perfectly in relationship to the observer.'

'At the risk of abusing your hospitality, professor, might I have another drink? My imagination is drying up.'

'Of course. You think I'm off my rocker, just like all the others.'

'Let's just say that, as in everything else, there's a gap between theory and practice. But what do your colleagues think of your ideas?'

Jelenski removed his glasses in order to wipe his forehead.

'I don't bother to talk to them.'

'Then what gives me that privilege?'

'You, my boy, are an artist. Coming out of your mouth, such a theory would inevitably be viewed as imaginative madness. And nobody could put it into practice without knowing the secrets of the plants.'

It was André's turn to wipe his brow. The air in the mill was oppressive. And in his mind, largely due to the effects of the third glass of whisky, he felt a kind of ambient madness spreading through the room. His host was so serious, and his logic so apparently reasonable, that he had to ask himself which one of the two had lost his mind. The heat, the whisky, the famous theories, the text of his play, there were a lot of things to consider.

'So you can see into the past, Mr. Jelinski?'

The astronomer, still looking like an old owl, answered him in a changed voice:

'In certain cases. Because I know where, when and how to look. And I can assure you that one sometimes sees the most astonishing things.'

17

A TALE OF COWBOYS

Narrative of Achilles Stock (continued)

January 11, 1911

That morning, around nine o'clock, in *The Two Crowns*, the only inn in Broomfield, Wedekind, Burns and I, who had taken rooms there, were comparing notes over a hearty breakfast. Wedekind had only picked at his, being absorbed by the latest developments in the investigation. The previous night, after both Owen and I had retired, an officer had brought Wedekind the dossier of the Miller affair. I could see he had made a summary, from the notes in his handwriting, next to a steaming cup of tea.

'What Bellamy said was correct,' he began, 'and he has a cast-iron alibi. It all happened on the eleventh of October, 1901, in Belgravia. A ten-year-old boy witnessed the scene from the window of his room in the house opposite 8, Crescent Alley—Jane Miller's address. It was ten o'clock at night and the rain was coming down in buckets. He saw Mrs. Miller coming back to her house, head down, empty-handed. Having seen her half an our earlier leaving her house and calling to her dog, he realised that her adored but disobedient pet had escaped from the house, which happened often. The old woman stopped suddenly just before arriving at her residence, looking at her house as if "turned into a pumpkin"—the boy's words. For Tommy—our young witness—neither her house, nor those of her neighbours had changed in any way. But, in truth, he couldn't see much through the rain on his window, except that the ground-floor lights were on.'

'Maybe they hadn't been when she went out,' suggested Owen thoughtfully.

'The dossier doesn't say. Be that as it may, he saw the widow bend down to look for something on the ground, then pass her arm through the railings. Tommy couldn't see what it was. In fact, it was a gold watch, belonging to the victim. We know that because it was found at that spot the next day. Then the woman turned round suddenly. Tommy didn't understand why at first, but when she started to run in the direction from which she'd come, he noticed a dark figure, coming from the other side of the street, following her rapidly. It was wearing a hat and a raincoat, that's all he could see behind the rain streaming down his window. He thought it was a man but, only having seen the figure from the back, it was only a supposition. The person was neither big nor small, that's all the kid was sure about. In any case it was evidently the widow's killer. Mrs. Miller was found slumped on the pavement a hundred yards away, at the exit of a covered alleyway. She had received a number of blows to the head, undoubtedly from a brick, because there was a pile of them on a nearby construction site. The medical examiner estimated the time of death at ten o'clock, which coincides with the boy's testimony. Is everything clear so far, gentlemen?'

'Perfectly,' said Owen, enjoying his bacon and eggs. 'But it's Daren Bellamy's famous alibi that we're waiting for.'

'Very well. So I'll move on to his relationship with the widow, for which we have his own testimony, already known, and that of several witnesses who observed his frequent visits to Mrs. Miller. It seems readily apparent that they weren't uniquely because of her beautiful eyes. On that night of the eleventh of October, from eight o'clock until midnight, Bellamy participated in a "country" evening in a restaurant in Soho, about ten minutes away from Crescent Alley. About fifty people, most of them disguised as cowboys. Not a masked ball, by any means. Rodeo wear: hat, scarf around the neck, that's about it. No fewer than twenty witnesses testified that Bellamy was there all night and was never absent for more than five minutes. And around ten o'clock he played the piano and sang for about an hour. In short, he had an iron-clad alibi. Without it, not only would he have not have inherited Mrs. Miller's wealth—her house and some savings—but he would have been good for the gallows. He already had a dubious past, being suspected of numerous thefts and confidence tricks, but had never been caught. So, what do you think, Burns?'

'We need more details in order to form a precise opinion.'

'I know the inspector who led the investigation, and he is still on the force. He will no doubt remember the case. We'll have the opportunity to talk to him. Anything else?'

'The alibi seems too good to be true.'

'And that's twice,' added the policeman, 'that he's been enjoying himself with friends whilst rich benefactors are being bumped off.'

'Quite. But in our present case, his alibi is far from being perfect. Is there anything new on the subject?'

'Some,' said Wedekind, clearly embarrassed. 'His gaming companions aren't just anybody. A handful of them are from the best families, notably the son of a member of parliament and the daughter of an influential banker... both of whom need to be approached tactfully. I had no idea that scoundrel kept such company. They were all playing cards in the back room of a pub in Piccadilly, and his alibi is good until one o'clock, when they separated. That's where it gets a bit bizarre. Bellamy claims he returned to his hotel and the others went home. But nobody in any of the cases can confirm it. From one o'clock on until the morning, nobody can account for their movements. Admittedly, the hour was late, but even so... It was the sergeant who interviewed all of them who made the observation, which seems well founded.'

'It is strange,' agreed Owen, 'but what in this case isn't, I ask you, Wedekind?'

The Scotland Yard inspector brought his fist down on the table hard enough to rattle the teacups.

'They're mocking us, Burns! I'm sure of it. And I can tell you that, with his inheritance at stake, and that sordid affair in his past, our gigolo friend won't escape so easily. This time he hasn't got a solid alibi. The heavy presumptions weighing on him will make the difference.'

'If it can be shown that Mrs. Sanders' death was murder, then yes. But for now that's not the case. Murderers, like everyone else, leave tracks when they walk on snow.'

'Suppose he had an accomplice?' I interjected. 'We haven't considered that.'

'For which crime?' replied Owen, with a smile. 'The first or the second?'

'Both.'

'You're thinking of professional hit-men, as our friends across the Atlantic call them?'

'Why not?'

'At the risk of surprising you, Achilles, I've already thought of that. But if that was the case, explain to me why Bellamy, when paying for the service, didn't order a better alibi for the death of his sister? And, at the risk of repeating myself, the murder theory remains unproven. The same goes for suicide. Even the most obtuse jury would find it hard to accept. One can't commit suicide by throwing oneself down in the snow.'

'That's all very well, Burns,' said the policeman testily. 'But let me remind you that you were the one who started us down that track with your story of the book which drives people mad, and your insistence that its presence in the victim's room couldn't be a coincidence.'

'I know, Wedekind,' replied my friend, running a hand nervously through his hair. 'It was just a way of saying that we were floundering lamentably, that everything seemed contradictory....'

'And, by the way, we still haven't found that book, and it's not from want of trying. One more thing: the autopsy report confirms that Mrs. Sanders did indeed die at around four in the morning, with a maximum margin of error of one hour either way.'

Wedekind was interrupted by the arrival of the publican, who told him he was wanted on the telephone.

When he returned a few minutes later, there was a grim look on his face.

'That was Andrew Johnson,' he muttered. 'He's just discovered Chandra's body in the drawing room.'

18

A VISIT FROM DR. MOREAU

July 19, 1991

After his smoke-filled and alcoholic meeting with the astronomer, which had lasted late into the night, André only got up when the sun was at its zenith. Célia was not there to greet him. He remembered it was her "Parisian" day and she had an important meeting to attend. In other words, she would be back late. At around two o'clock the doorbell rang. He was surprised to find Dr. Moreau standing there for, as it happened, he had been planning to pay him a visit.

But this time the roles were reversed. André was at home, in his own armchair with lions' heads on the armrests, indicating clearly who was the master of the house. Dr. Moreau, who was on the sofa, looked around like a domestic cat suddenly thrown into a jungle. The comparison was excessive, but he was visibly not at ease. Even though the heat of the day was not at its maximum, his bald pate was already moist and he rubbed his hands incessantly.

'Mme. Lévêque isn't here today?' he asked, trying to appear natural.

'No, she's in Paris. She goes there once or twice a week for her work.'

'I understand, I understand. It's strange, I've been here a couple of times to bring cassettes, but I don't even know her name.'

'I might be able to help you there,' replied André drily, lighting a cigarette. 'Her name's Célia.'

The psychoanalyst took a deep breath and tried to smile:

'Célia, that's a pretty name. Excuse me, do you have anything to drink? I came here on foot and the sun is quite hot.'

'I'm sorry, what would you like? A cold beer? A whisky?'

'A large glass of water, if you please.'

A few moments later, having slaked his thirst, he began:

'I've been thinking about this business again, André... and I'm afraid we've taken another wrong turn.'

'Don't tell me it's about the film. There's no doubt in my mind about that.'

'No, that's settled. I was thinking about Rita and all my rantings about her and her entourage.'

'So she's not implicated in any crime?'

'No, I'd be really surprised if she were. She might have had a relationship with the father of your friend, but as far as the rest is concerned, I think we went too far. We allowed our imagination to get the better of us and made her into a diabolical criminal. And it's all my fault, I admit. Your case was particularly interesting and you seemed so distraught... I wanted to help, but in so doing I lost my professional objectivity. Anyway, I came here to say that it's pointless to annoy that woman again. Better still, forget about the whole business and hang on to our success.'

'Which was to see the invisible.'

'Excuse me?'

'Thanks to you, I've been able to see *The Unseen* again, which is about an invisible murderer.'

'Ah, yes,' said Dr. Moreau, with an approving smile. 'But, in fact, what did you think of the film itself? According to Ronald Lecourbe, the expert who unearthed that copy, it's workmanlike, but nothing more, and I tend to agree.'

'Well I don't! It's dazzling from beginning to end. It creates an atmosphere of fear in the most subtle manner.'

'That's the ten-year-old boy talking, I take it?'

'Of course. The film made too much of an impression for me to be impartial.'

After taking a large swig of the whisky he'd just served himself, André added pensively:

'I'm willing to accept that we fantasized too much, that Rita is perfectly innocent, and that Mme. Lamblin's death was nothing but an accident. But what troubles me is that I now believe I'm personally involved in the affair.'

'Which affair? The film or the accident?'

'The film. The house in the rain, the white staircase, the gold fob watch and all the rest of it. I feel I know those things intimately.'

Leaning back in the sofa with a finger on his lips, Dr. Moreau declared after a silence:

'I understand, and we've now reverted to our original hypothesis, which I believe to be the right one. In fact, I'd come to the same conclusion as you, but hadn't wanted to say so, for fear of perturbing you more. But since you realised yourself... We have to envisage a phenomenon of metempsychosis. I'm not an expert in the domain—which isn't recognised officially by scientists—but is it more difficult to accept as a principle of nature than rain in springtime? Anyway, I was struck by the power of your memories, by the images and their obsessive nature. Everything came from deep within.'

'So I lived a previous life?' asked André, staring at the bottom of his glass, as if it held the answer to his question.

Dr. Moreau shrugged his shoulders:

'That's one explanation, and I admit I can't see any other. That being the case, let me give my final advice: forget all that. You've solved the main puzzle, identifying the film, and you've surmounted the obstacle which prevented you from writing, which was the essential. Everything else can be cast aside. Don't bother digging up the past—nothing good ever comes of it. And forget Rita, she can't help you.'

After the psychoanalyst had left, André returned to his armchair, served himself another drink, and tried to think. Too many thoughts were rattling around in his head for him to form a calm analysis. And on top of everything else there was the new play he'd just finished. It was like adding lemon juice to a drink which was already too acid. The psychoanalyst's game was only too clear and quite predictable, but something wasn't right. Dr. Moreau hadn't convinced him that Rita had nothing to do with it... He tried to reconcile the information at his disposal, but the king in his latest play, dressed in yellow rags, perturbed his thoughts.

War-weary he got up and went to his wife's office. He opened a drawer of the dresser and took out an old mauve notebook. Underneath was a pile of photos. The one on the top was of his friend Guy, who must have been twelve or thirteen at the time. He was holding his sister, who was sitting on a swing. After looking at the snapshot for a few moments, André shrugged his shoulders and returned to the drawing room with the mauve notebook in his hand.

***

Célia came back at half-past nine. Even though she was tired, she was eager to hear his latest news. André described his night at the mill and Dr. Moreau's surprise visit in detail.

'You say he was very nervous, darling?'

'To say the least. But he regained his confidence at the end and advised me to bury that old story for good.'

'How I would have loved to have been there!' exclaimed Célia.

'He also strongly discouraged me from seeing Rita again.'

'There, he's probably right. Is it still necessary?'

'I almost want to go, just to spite him.'

'And I, darling, would like to meet Professor Jelenski, to visit the mill and watch the stars with him!'

'He's an old loony, but logical enough in his ramblings. I confess that up there in his lair, with his huge telescope, through which I could see marvellous nebulae to the accompaniment of his erudite commentary, the magic started to operate. Accompanied by some good whisky... I started to believe his crackpot theories.'

'I should have come with you. But I wasn't bored last night either.'

'Ah? And who entertained you in my absence?'

'You did. You see, I'm a faithful wife.'

'Well, we've had reincarnation and invisible colours allowing us to see the past, so I suppose bilocation shouldn't come as a surprise.'

'I meant your spirit, not your person.'

'Ah! Thought transference....'

'I read your play.'

André stiffened. He looked at his wife, then lowered his eyes.

'You shouldn't have done. I'd hidden it.'

'Well, not well enough. I must say it's a long way from what you normally do. It's... I thought about it the whole day with shivers, despite the heat. I admit I didn't understand what you were trying to say. There are moments when it's deranged and detestable. And I ask myself whom it's supposed to please....'

'You shouldn't have read it, Célia,' André repeated nervously. 'My objective wasn't necessarily to make it public.'

'Then what was it?'

'I wanted to prove something to myself. After such a long absence, I needed to touch the listener at his deepest core.'

'Well, you certainly succeeded!'

As André seemed to lose himself in thought, Célia continued:

'Listen, it's not a judgment about its merits. The quality of the writing is undeniable, perhaps the best you've done....'

After taking a few paces, she continued:

'The first act is conventional enough, but from the beginning of the second act, it grips you. I literally lived the scenes.' A distant look came into her eyes. 'The one where the inhabitants of the two rival towns, united in front of the royal palace to hear Queen Cassilda sing from her balcony, sing the song of reconciliation in her marvellous voice.... And when the emotion is at its height and the spectators are crying tears of joy after having found a harmony they had thought lost forever, Queen Cassilda throws herself off the balcony and into the void! The thud of her fall chills every heart... And then the beautiful Camilla throws herself on the body of the one she held so dear... But instead of crying her heart out, she suddenly bursts into laughter... a laugh so hideous the entire crowd is frozen in terror... The twin suns have disappeared from the horizon... The moon rises in front of the distant towers... The baleful light reveals the man in the pale mask who has just appeared. We think he wants to help Camilla and cure her of her madness by offering her a helping hand, but his grip is so firm that the young woman's finger becomes detached from her hand... and that's just the beginning.'

19

A CAST-IRON ALIBI

Narrative of Achilles Stock (continued)

The sky was perfectly clear that morning. The weather was magnificent, enhanced by the glare from the snow. The brilliant light which permeated the drawing room of Raven Lodge bathed the body of Chandra Ganesh, lying in front of the fireplace, in a golden light, as if to underline the contrast with the macabre scene we were contemplating, Wedekind, Owen and I, having rapidly abandoned our breakfast at the pub. Chandra was lying on his stomach, his arms slightly apart and his head near the stone base of the hearth. There was a deep contusion on his left temple.

'The perpetual battle between day and night,' I commented gravely. 'Between good and evil. Death has profited from complicit shadows to extract a new tribute, before flying away with a loud flapping of wings, like a bat fleeing the light.'

'Ah, the famous wings of death,' exclaimed Owen, who was ferreting around by the hearth. 'Cursed be they! If we could tear them once and for all from the Grim Reaper... That would be very practical, Achilles, don't you think?'

'Maybe not,' I replied. 'You would soon be out of a job.'

'A better observation than the first, Achilles. You get back the point you lost.'

Ignoring our banter, Wedekind growled with a bitter smile:

'Someone else who had a bad fall. It's become a habit around here.'

'So, do you have another explanation?' asked Owen. 'And if so, what is it based on?'

'On everything,' said the policeman, irritably. 'And I'm not in the mood to appreciate your attempts at humour. I can see at least two or three heavy objects in the room which could have been used to inflict the mortal blow to the temple. Positioning the head of the victim close to the base of the hearth to make believe it was a fall was fatuous.

Only a dumb detective from a detective novel would fall for that. I'm surprised that such a distinguished detective as yourself hasn't ruled it out immediately.'

'Then I take it you haven't noticed anything else, Wedekind. Very well, start by looking at the tips of the fingers, particularly of the right hand. They're black from fumes. Then examine the hearth. You too, Achilles.'

After we had done so, without result, he added:

'The ashes, gentlemen, the ashes. They're not natural, at least in their arrangement. It's not clear at first glance, but to an eye as experienced as mine, it's obvious. You still don't see it? The edges are curiously free. Someone worked hard to pile them up in the middle of the hearth. To do that late at night, when the fire is left to die before going to bed, is pretty unusual, I'd say. So the fire was piled like that in order to burn something, to make an object that Chandra was holding in his hand disappear. An object that was more or less consumed, judging by his blackened fingers. By Zeus, if there were only a few traces somewhere!' He said this whilst on all fours in pursuit of his frantic investigation.

A moment later, leaning over the tool bucket, he let out an "Eureka" fit to shatter eardrums. After removing poker, tongs and brush, he emptied the contents of the bucket gingerly on the tiles.

'There, gentlemen,' he announced triumphantly. 'Look, there's a small piece of cardboard and some bits of paper, consumed at the edges. I'll warrant Chandra was holding them when he was brutally attacked. Otherwise, how could they have landed here? It looks like the corner of a book, wouldn't you say? From the bit of cardboard, the cover, we can tell its colour....'

'Yellow,' declared Wedekind darkly. 'Yellow, as in *The King in Yellow* we've been looking for so assiduously. By golly, I'm beginning to understand. Someone was taking advantage of the darkness to make the book disappear forever in the embers. Chandra Ganesh must have surprised them.'

'Yes, and out of curiosity he started to sift through the embers, noticed the remains of the yellow book and tried to preserve them. That's when our unknown assailant hit him over the head with the first heavy object that came to hand. In their haste to throw the remains back into the fire, they failed to notice that a tiny portion had fallen into the tool bucket. None of this tells us their identity, of course, but it does show how desperate they were to destroy the book. And that's where it gets interesting, gentlemen.'

He paused to let that sink in, then continued:

'What is the precise reason for this initiative? I can see two possible hypotheses. The first is that they wanted to rid humanity of that harmful book.'

'They wouldn't have killed the Indian if that were the case.'

'Precisely. So the book is a fake. By that I meant isn't even a real work, the fruit of a crazed author. It was simply created by our assailant from some play or other and enclosed in a yellow cover. Which leads me to my second hypothesis....'

'But,' I interjected. 'We suspected that already.'

'Yes, but now it's a certainty. It's no longer a book selected by Mrs. Sanders, who squirreled it away who knows where. All the shenanigans regarding the book were carefully planned and premeditated. And premeditation means assassination.'

'Double assassination,' added Wedekind grimly.

'We've been led up the garden path, so to speak, and had sand thrown in our eyes. Far-fetched though it was, the idea that Mrs. Sanders, distressed and unsteady, fled into the snow to escape the throes of a nightmare was burnt into our brains. With the disturbing figure of the cursed king, draped in yellow rags pursuing the unfortunate woman, dazed and dishevelled... What a beautifully dramatic picture, don't you think? It's clear we're dealing with a subtle adversary, an artist.'

'Quite,' said the inspector tersely. 'But enough of the lyricism. The noose is tightening around our joker. I can't wait to talk to him.'

'Keep the best till last, Wedekind. There's no point in rushing things now we're getting close.'

Apart from my friend's deductions, nothing important arose during our questioning. Andrew, the first to get up, but still half asleep, had found the body when he went into the drawing room. He was the last person to have seen Chandra alive, as well, having crossed him in the corridor at around eleven o'clock as he was going to bed. He hadn't noticed anything unusual in the other's attitude. After dinner, Alice had had a philosophical discussion with Chandra whilst contemplating the stars. What he'd said was largely mysterious and impenetrable, so she hadn't taken it literally. Cheryl and Daren had also seen him around in the house, but before eleven. Everyone claimed to have been in their room after that time, and to have fallen asleep rapidly. No one had heard any suspicious noises during the night.

In mid-afternoon, we called Daren Bellamy into the room, in the presence of two police officers. Tensions had risen a notch, even though the body had been taken away by then. According to the medical examiner, Chandra died around one o'clock in the morning, due toa blow from a blunt instrument. The possibility of a fall against the hearth could not be ruled out, but only from a "purely theoretical" point of view, he stressed.

Wedekind led the questioning. After lighting a cigar, he laid out the serious charges which might be laid against him, forcefully evoking in considerable detail the savage murder of the widow Miller. Bellamy remained quiet. Then the inspector underlined the astonishing similarities between the two affairs, with their "festive" alibis, in particular the second, with its hole of five hours, covering the moment of Mrs. Sanders' death, looking particularly suspect. After that, he brought up the "affair of the yellow book", in which he went into detail about our latest conclusions, which had the effect of wiping Bellamy's arrogant smirk off his face for an instant.

'Do me a favour, inspector, and stop this idiocy about *The King in Yellow*! We're not children any more. Nobody's with you on this. It's a joke!'

'Not for Mr. Ganesh, it wasn't. He, as it's been proven, was killed because of it. You committed a grave error in lowering your vigilance at that moment, when the piece of cardboard fluttered into the bucket. But it was understandable, you'd just committed a murder. And not the first, I may add.'

'Very well,' said Bellamy abruptly, his eyes gleaming. 'I'll put my cards on the table. It's what you wanted, and it's what you're going to get. During that five-hour hole in my alibi, as you call it, in other words, after our game of cards, I was still with my friends Phillip and Charlotte. They're married, as you know, but not to each other officially.'

'I know who they are, thank you.'

'But, unofficially, it looks like it. At the *Red Dragon*, a shady joint close by which we visit frequently, there are all kinds of lascivious and exotic entertainments. We stayed there the rest of the night. To implicate them any further would greatly embarrass them and ruin our friendship. And you, inspector, would risk having your wings clipped in the process.'

Twenty-four hours later, we had confirmation of Bellamy's claims. The owner and his Asiatic employees remembered him and his friends. The friends themselves confirmed Bellamy's alibi, although it required all of Wedekind's tact and promises of discretion. Bellamy probably lost his friends, but not his head. He was cleared of all suspicion in the death of Mrs. Sanders, and consequently for Chandra's also, on the grounds of there being only one criminal, if there was indeed one at all. His alibi was henceforth cast-iron.

20

RETURN TO BRITTANY

July 25, 1991

Night was falling on the Brittany countryside. André had long ago given up hope of arriving at a decent hour, having been stopped for a long time by an accident on the motorway. He had no choice but to find a hotel for the night. Which was beginning to look harder and harder the farther he was from Rennes. He drove through hamlets which seemed straight out of another age, and others which appeared deserted. Only the crosses, which raised their sombre silhouettes at crossroads, seemed familiar. He had written to Rita the day after Dr. Moreau's visit, in his most winning manner, to ask for another appointment. Just as before, her response—which he had not been counting on—was rapid. She told him, however, that he had better hurry if he wanted to see her, for she was on the point of absenting herself for several days. Would he find the door closed the next day, he worried? He was starting to feel dangerously tired and fearful of falling asleep at the wheel.

The wind had just become stronger. He felt his car starting to sway. The leaves on the trees began to rustle. The horizon was a red gash. That was when he saw *it*, clad in yellow and wearing a hood. It was crossing the road, indifferent to the vehicles bearing down on it. André stamped on the brakes. His car swerved and he controlled it with difficulty. He turned the engine off, stepped out of the car, and was buffeted by the wind, bringing a beneficial freshness. He couldn't see anyone. And for good reason, the figure had only existed in his mind. Not for the first time, either. André smiled. The King in Yellow must not have appreciated being revived in a play, particularly one which cast him in such an unfavourable light.

His hair dishevelled by the wind, his raincoat clinging to his body, lost on the wild moors, André felt his strength waning. In the wailing of the wind he could hear Cassilda singing...the song of harmony which had transformed into nightmare... he thought about Célia. Had it been wise to leave her alone in the house at such a critical time? She managed to make light of things, but he knew that inside she was bursting with impatience. And she had become visibly more nervous since the visit of Dr. Moreau. Unless it was because of his play? What stupidity not to have hidden it better. He would have preferred to have shown it to her in its finished form, more nuanced, less brutal. The first version, because of its gratuitous violence, gave a bad impression of its author which would be hard to overcome. That is what he would have liked to avoid. For him, it had been just a simple exercise in style, nothing more. Cassilda, the masked man, Camilla, the King in Yellow were just fictional characters. And he certainly wasn't going to meet them here, in this lost corner of Brittany. Their home was in the town of Carcosa, in the Hyades, where the star Aldebaran shone, many light-years away.

From her balcony, drowning out the howling of the wind, Cassilda continued to sing, before throwing herself suddenly into the void... André thought about Jeanne Langlois—alias Janine Lamblin—who had taken a similar plunge from the edge of the old quarry. Assuredly pushed by criminal hands.... But how? And by whom? He was no longer sure of the identity of the culprit. Suppose it was Camille herself? Or the King in Yellow? Or the stranger in the pale mask?

***

The following day, at around ten o'clock, André was again taking coffee with Rita Messmer in the arbour. He had spent an uncomfortable night on the back seat of his car, but had now recovered through the miracle of black coffee. The phantom characters of the night had been chased away by the first rays of dawn.

'You're lucky to find me here, André. I'm leaving tomorrow,' said Rita, lighting yet another cigarette.

'Send me away whenever you like.'

'You mustn't have made this journey in vain. You must stay for lunch, even though I can only offer you an omelette.'

'You're too kind, madam.'

'You know,' she continued, 'it gives me great pleasure to talk about

126

the past. A painful past, certainly, but an eventful one with plenty of surprises and fleeting moments of happiness.'

'I have the same impression, at least for the past happiness. As a child, making new discoveries every day, it was a wonderfully carefree time.'

'So did you come here in search of lost happiness?' asked Rita in a voice tinged with irony.

'To a degree, yes. But not just for that. I'd like to believe my wife when she says I have a lot of qualities, but I know I have a lot of faults.'

'Like everyone.'

'And one of them is curiosity. My biggest problem is that I abhor mysteries. As a child, the mere view of a masked enemy, even in children's comic books made me shiver and bubble with curiosity.'

'I suppose you want to go back over that painful business,' sighed his hostess.

'Yes, madam, I won't deny it. I can't explain exactly why, but there's a good reason for it. How can I put it, someone's happiness is at stake.'

'I'm all ears.'

'I'll start with the episode of Mme. Langlois' watch. She gave it to you because it never worked, and regretted it afterwards.'

'I only found out quite a bit later, from Jean-Pierre's own mouth. But he also advised me not to go back, because his wife would be upset.'

'You wore the watch as a medallion, I've heard.'

'Yes, given that it wasn't useful for anything else. Nevertheless, I actually stopped wearing it when I heard that it had been the subject of a violent quarrel. But is it so important?'

'Only for the memory. Because I seem to remember you wore a pendant just like it at the time.'

'Well then, you have a phenomenal memory, André!' exclaimed Rita smilingly. 'If that's the case, you can have it.'

'Is it still in your possession?'

'Yes. But I should have got rid of it a long time ago. Not only had it never worked, it didn't bring me any luck either.'

A few minutes later, the young playwright was holding it in his hands. Contemplating it, he observed:

127

'Truthfully, if it hadn't been for the film I might not have remembered that you wore it.'

'What a shame. I thought for a moment that it was because of my personality.'

'That also, I'm sure. Your long black hair always—.'

'Stop talking to me about my hair. It's too painful a subject for me!'

'Unfortunately I have to address another, intimately tied to your personal charm.'

'You intrigue me.'

'Without beating about the bush: did you have a relationship with Jean-Pierre Langlois at the time?'

There was a silence, broken by the sound of a passing moped.

'Yes,' she said eventually. 'A long, passionate relationship,'

'And all the more passionate for being secret.'

'Like all impossible love affairs. But I thought you'd read my mind the last time you were here,' said Rita Messmer, adjusting her tinted glasses.

'More or less, but I wanted to be sure. And did Mme. Langlois know?'

'No, I don't think so. I don't think she suspected anything. She was too anxious about life in general. She was very nervous by nature. She stuffed herself with tranquilisers and drank excessively— sometimes to the point of having hallucinations. She had a phobia about bats and saw them everywhere. She couldn't handle daily life.'

'Didn't she see a specialist?'

'Several of them. The last one did get some results, but it didn't last. She inspired pity, and that was our problem. Jean-Pierre and I couldn't bring ourselves to speak to her frankly. We thought it might be too much for her psychologically.'

'But what happened after her disappearance?'

With a wry smile, Rita replied:

'Why didn't we marry, now that we were free, is that what you mean?' André nodded. 'The tragedy destroyed us. Neither Jean-Pierre nor I were ever the same afterwards. The worst suspicions hung over us during the investigation. We were eventually cleared, thank goodness, but the damage had been done. Our relationship continued, with the greatest discretion, needless to say. But the ghost of Jeanne haunted us every time we embraced. Every time I looked into Jean-

Pierre's eyes, I saw his wife's accusing look. It reached the point where I couldn't even look at him, it was horrible... We had to end our relationship, even though we were still in love with each other.'

In the silence which followed, Rita wiped away the tears streaming down her cheeks. She swallowed and continued:

'It was the worst moment of my life... And I never recovered.'

21

THE DEPARTURE

January 13, 1911

After having closed her voluminous suitcase, Cheryl Chapman took one last look in the mirror, which reflected the image she expected to see. She reflexively adopted a model's pose, adjusting her hat, placing a hand under her chin and smiling at herself. Even her thick coat could not hide her graceful curves. Daren would be proud of her. Daren, who was undoubtedly waiting for her in the drawing room, ready to leave this sinister, isolated place. No, she wasn't being fair. Raven Lodge was also the place where they met. Or, more precisely, the train taking them there, which would also take them back to London after a weekend that had been extended because of the investigation. But she was finished here. At least in her eyes, since the police had finally accepted that Daren had had nothing to do with the tragic event. There was a new life ahead of her, as bright as the shining snow she could see out of the window. It wasn't the first time her life had taken a radical turn, but she was sure this was it. So much effort could not help but pay a dividend. Needless to say, she wouldn't be keeping her position as secretary. She'd thought about it, but not for long. She hadn't told Andrew yet, but it wouldn't be long. She'd think about it some more on the train.

In a nearby room, Alice Johnson was sizing herself up in the mirror, but more briefly than had Cheryl. Like her, she was thinking about the future with confidence and optimism, although more cautiously. With a strange smile, she wondered if she had any reason to complain, with a husband who was now the director of the company... Andrew, who had just left the room with their bags. He hadn't stopped consulting his watch at the window, awaiting the carriage which was to take them to the station. When he eventually left, with an imperious "don't be too late", it had been a blessed relief. He was getting harder and harder to tolerate. His desire to leave the place had turned into an obsession within the last twenty-four hours. He wanted to leave "this sinister place" as quickly as possible. Certainly the dramatic events were a good enough reason, but she wasn't fooled for a moment. She knew what was eating at him. And the idea that Daren would now be profiting from his sister's death certainly hadn't helped.

A quick look at the clock told her that it was half-past nine and time to leave, to quit Raven Lodge for good, along with its ghosts, destined to haunt it forever. Chandra's serene face swam into her vision. She would miss him, his wisdom and his calm assurance. She'd thought for a long time about their conversation under the stars. What had he wanted to say exactly? Why had he given her the glue he'd made, as if it was an essential part of her future?

A few minutes later, Daren, Cheryl and the Johnsons, together with their dog, were installed in the small horse-drawn omnibus taking them to the station. Nobody spoke. Each seemed absorbed in contemplation of the snow-covered landscape. Once on the train, they separated into two groups, Alice resolutely choosing a different compartment from Daren and Cheryl.

An hour later they met again on the platform of Charing Cross station. Some were smiling, others not. Daren, in the first category, declared that it was the moment for them to part, perhaps never to meet again, and that the trials they had just shared had served to underline the radiant future which awaited them. Andrew muttered an inaudible response, whereas Alice remained impassive. Cheryl, who was also part of the first category, threw herself in Andrew's arms as if overcome by tenderness, and announced:

'Thanks for everything, Andrew. I haven't told you yet, but I've decided to leave the Sanders company.'

'Really?' said Alice sourly. 'What a surprise!'

'Yes, really,' continued Cheryl, affecting a contrite air. 'I've thought about it for a long time. It's not a decision I've taken lightly. I owe you a lot, and I won't forget...*we've passed such wonderful moments together.*'

Andrew went pale and Alice seemed to have been turned into stone.

'Thank you for everything, Andrew,' continued Cheryl, batting her eyelashes and clinging to Daren's arm. 'You've helped me and guided me almost like a father, but now I've found someone else to take care of me. I wish you both a happy future.'

On the way home, and up to the moment they reached their London flat, the Johnsons said not a word. Then Alice found her tongue and unleashed a tirade very much unlike her:

'How could she dare, the little bitch! Humiliating you like that in public. I was ashamed for you, Andrew. And you didn't even react! She deserved a hundred times over the slap you never gave her. Not to mention me... I hope you realise it was very offensive for me as well. No, I can see that doesn't bother you at all. If she came back tomorrow to say she'd changed her mind, you would take her back in a heartbeat.'

'Certainly not, darling,' said Andrew, trying to reassure her.

'Don't call me that ever again. It's meaningless.'

So saying, she turned on her heel and slammed the door in his face. Andrew could hear her sobs behind the closed door.

The following day, she kept her silence. Even when Hector barked, she didn't react. And the day after that, when Andrew returned from work, he was surprised to see an armada of suitcases in their drawing room. Alice, in an armchair, seemed absorbed with her embroidery.

'What's happening?' he stammered, his eyes wide open. 'Have you decided to take some time away?'

'Yes,' she replied laconically.

'Well, maybe it's not such a bad idea, after all we've been through.'

'I'm taking time away permanently, Andrew. Enough is enough.'

22

THE MILL

It was after ten o'clock when André and Célia left their domicile. It was a magnificent night, just like the previous ones. The warm, fragrant air was an invitation to stroll in contemplation of the firmament and the myriads of twinkling stars. Whilst the couple made their way towards the old mill on the gently-climbing powdery path, André thought about his visit the previous day to Rita, which he had only partially described to his wife. Célia continued to insist on the futility of the trip, as she'd predicted, but André wasn't so sure. The confirmation of the secret liaison between Rita and Jean-Pierre Langlois and the disturbed nature of Janine, which had not previously been known, shed a new light on the matter. On the other hand, he wasn't sure that Célia's initiative was going to be a success. She had insisted that he take her chez Jelenski to see the stars. Given that the astronomer had invited him to drop by whenever the skies appeared to be favourable, he hadn't thought it necessary to notify him in advance. Célia had seemed to be as happy as a child all day long, but from time to time the laughter in her eyes turned into distant stares, betraying some inner torment. And she'd made a couple of strange remarks about the play. Something wasn't right, he could sense it.

'I can't wait to see all those marvels in the telescope,' she said, raising her eyes to the sky.

'We're almost there.'

'By the way, darling, have you seen Christine lately?'

'No, I don't think so. Why do you ask?'

'It's been quite some time since I've seen her doing her shopping in the village.'

'She may be on a trip.'

'That's true. She goes away a lot. Some people have all the luck.'

The dark silhouette of the mill soon loomed up against the dark blue velvet of the sky. So far, everything had gone well. After André pressed the doorbell, they anticipated a warm welcome from the spirited old astronomer. It was not to be the case.

'Oh, it's you,' he said, unenthusiastically and obviously in surprise.

'If we've come at a bad time....' said Célia.

'No, come in. The sky won't be as clear tomorrow. Better make the most of it.'

A few moments later, whilst Célia was lavishing compliments on the layout and decoration of the place, he invited them without further comment to follow him to the observatory. The astronomer adjusted the telescope and gave the same commentary as he had done before, but with much less enthusiasm. Which didn't prevent Célia from uttering enthusiastic cries as she contemplated the nebulae of Lagoon and Trifid.

'It's splendid! I'm sure that Carcosa is around here somewhere.'

'No,' replied André, 'it's in the Hyades, which we can't see today.'

'I'm sure it's here,' she cried exultantly. 'I can see the towers of the town, and Lake Hali.'

Carl Jelenski frowned.

'And there's the palace! And I can see a woman on the balcony. It must be Cassilda, I'm sure of it. Next door to her is a man in a mask... or else it's the King in Yellow himself!'

Pushing her cavalierly out of the way, the astronomer scrutinised the sky through the telescope. Then he shrugged his shoulders. André intervened to explain that his wife was making joking references to his play.

'I don't like that sort of joke,' growled Jelenski. 'Particularly coming from people like you.'

Whilst Célia maintained her ironic smile, André replied tersely:

'I'm afraid I don't understand.'

'And I,' retorted the professor, fixing him with an owl-like stare, 'know that you understand very well.'

There was a deathly silence. The cold determination in the astronomer's stare incited André to prudence.

'If you would be good enough to explain....'

The hoped-for calm did not happen. Jelenski pointed to each of them in turn with an accusing finger:

'I know what you did. I saw you the other night, in the snow.'

'In the snow?' repeated André. 'What are you talking about?'

'You were moving a body. And it was you. I recognised your faces.'

'A body?' asked André. 'Have you lost your mind? Get a hold of yourself, man.'

'It wasn't chance,' continued the professor, his face flushed. 'The initiate didn't place the colour there for nothing.'

'Ah!' exclaimed André, raising his arms in the air. 'I think I understand.'

Turning to his wife, with a discreet wink, he told her:

'It's the famous colour I told you about the other day. Do you remember, the colour that lets you see things which happened in the past? The professor must have made a new observation of the sort, and seen two suspect figures from another age, whom he thought had faces resembling ours. It's not the first time he's had success with such an experiment, because he believes that....'

'I didn't think I saw! It was you! And stop talking to me as if I'm an idiot.'

Célia, who had remained calm, gave the scientist an enigmatic smile.

'I don't think you're that, Professor Jelinski. Not only are you not mad, as you seem to want to make us believe, you're actually very cunning. Let's see, does the name Messmer mean anything to you? No? What about Heinrich Messmer? Still no? I think you have a very bad memory.'

This time it was the owl's eyes which widened in astonishment:

'What are you talking about?'

'You know very well. And stop this game of inverse accusation. If you think I don't understand your little game....'

Faced with the intense regard of the young woman, Jelinski capitulated:

'I don't think we've anything left to talk about.'

'I don't think so either.'

'I'll lead you back.'

'That's an excellent idea. After you!'

In the suffocating air under the roof beams, overheated by the day's sun, Carl Jelenski walked towards the staircase. As he started down the steep steps, Célia followed close behind, her hands out in front of her.

23

THE LAST CHANCE

Narrative of Achilles Stock (continued)

February, 1911

This account of events relies principally on the confidences of my friend, partly because I myself was occupied with personal matters related to my fine pottery business in the Cotswolds, and partly because Owen kept me at a distance regarding certain manoeuvres "necessitating solitary intervention" according to him. I only saw him occasionally, therefore, when I returned to the capital.

That is how I followed the elements of an investigation which, it must be admitted, had somewhat lost interest in my eyes. For Mrs. Sanders' demise, as for Chandra Ganesh's, the coroner's jury had returned a verdict of accidental death. We had reason to doubt that, but as far as I was concerned that impression became weaker over time.

Owen had informed me, meanwhile, that Alice Johnson had left her husband and was temporarily living in a hotel. As she scarcely had any family, the scandal affected only her husband's. According to Owen, who had met her, she had displayed courage and a rare determination. Whether her husband consented to a divorce or not, she had decided never to see him again, despite her precarious new situation.

On another occasion, he had informed me that he'd had a discussion with the inspector in charge of the Miller case, who remembered the question of Daren's alibi very well. He'd been frustrated, because he'd been convinced, particularly at the start of the investigation, of Bellamy's guilt. But, faced with the multiple testimonies in the suspect's favour, he'd had to defer to the facts.

'But what do you think, Owen?' I asked. 'I get the impression you have an idea in the back of your head.'

'Yes, Achilles. The inspector's detailed descriptions, and the archives, have given me a few ideas. We'll talk about it another time. That said, whatever the truth of the past case, it is not connected to the case of Mrs. Sanders.'

'In other words, Bellamy could be guilty in one case but not the other?'

'Precisely. Cases lumped together can be the worst enemy of our profession. And you know better than anyone that I'm too experienced to fall into that trap.'

Around the middle of February, Owen announced that he'd seen Cheryl Chapman again. A painter friend, who gave drawing classes, told him about a model he'd just hired with the same name. Owen had attended one of his classes.

'She's still just as pretty, Achilles,' he confided.

'I imagine one doesn't change much in three weeks. So she's renewed contact with the world of art. Surprising, isn't it?'

'Indeed. I offered her a cup of tea after the sitting. To cut a long story short, she's not seeing Daren Bellamy any more. I know that you thought they'd got off to a good start, but their beautiful romance ended quite rapidly. After two weeks, he'd decided they weren't meant for each other.'

'What an odious individual! But I'm not totally surprised... And it's sad for her.'

'She was upset, there's no doubt. But she's quite tough. Don't worry about her, Achilles. She has a certain experience of life, and I told her she could count on me for help. We promised to see each other again.'

'You're all heart, Burns. Your offer of help is so touching.'

The following week, Owen came to see me in my London flat, cheeks flushed with excitement. He declared straight out that human ingenuity, in the realm of crime, continued to surprise him, despite his long experience of the subject. Upon which, he embarked on a long list of classic cases perpetrated by particularly cunning criminals.

'Where are you going with this?' I finally asked. 'I know all about these cases.'

'We've been tricked, Achilles. We've had the wool royally pulled over our eyes.'

'Concerning the Sanders affair?' I guessed.

'Of course!' he replied in astonishment. 'I thought you'd understood.'

'In other words, Mrs. Sanders was indeed murdered.'

'Precisely. Now I'm absolutely certain of it.'

'But how?' I exclaimed. 'How did the murderer manage to approach her without leaving any traces in the snow?'

'The details aren't clear yet, but I'm beginning to have an idea.'

'More likely you're trying to keep me in suspense.'

'No, Achilles. I've only a rough idea at the moment. There's no doubt that it's an ingenious method, but it's not the main trick. For me, the trap was elsewhere, a psychological trap we fell for, hook line and sinker. Great art, Achilles, which inspires respect. Patience, I'll explain it all at the right time. But I'm hesitant about what might happen next....'

***

His bowler hat pulled down over his eyes and his back slightly hunched, Owen Burns crossed Great Russell Street and went into the tea-shop *Tattle and Tea* with a preoccupied air. Although it wasn't the most upper-crust establishment in London, Owen appreciated its audacious interior, its forest of pictures judiciously disposed throughout the room, and the purple colour of its paintings. But for now he seemed not to pay them attention. Nor to anything or anyone else. After sitting down at a table, he pulled a newspaper out of his pocket and unfolded it noisily before plunging his nose into it, ignoring his neighbours as if he were the only person in the world. It was a far from discreet entrance, which is exactly what he wanted. After a moment, he threw down his newspaper in obvious disgust, as if struck by some bad news. Looking darkly around, he stopped suddenly, his expression transfigured at the sight of a couple at a nearby table.

'Well, for heaven's sake,' he exclaimed. 'Mrs. Johnson... and Mr. Bellamy. What a coincidence!'

With an expression of agreeable surprise—although somewhat less than Owen's—they greeted the detective.

'The king of detectives in person,' said Daren Bellamy, with his perpetual dimpled smile. 'How nice to see you again, how are you?'

'May I join you?'

'Of course. We'd be vexed if you didn't.'

'What a surprise!' exclaimed Owen, sitting down. 'I might even say a double surprise. To see you here, and together. I thought that—.'

'I understand. But one must never say "fountain, I will never drink your water," must one, Alice?'

Mrs. Johnson agreed, with an embarrassed smile.

'I'm delighted to see you again, Mr. Burns. I haven't forgotten our last meeting, your compassion, and your comforting advice. You were the only one to react that way.'

'Not exactly,' interjected Daren mischievously.

Whereupon, Bellamy explained to Owen that he, too, after having run into Alice by chance, and having learnt of her situation, had comforted her—or at least tried—by offering her financial aid. All he had received in return was a stinging slap.

He put a hand to his cheek, as if he felt a retroactive pain.

'And?' prompted Owen, looking very intrigued.

'And, Mr. Burns,' said Alice, shooting him a look from her beautiful blue eyes, 'something strange happened. I didn't regret slapping the author of a proposition I found extremely offensive. But then the memory of my husband reared up in front of me and I had an idea. Suppose I threw myself into the arms of the person he considered his enemy since little Cheryl escaped? Could one imagine a more delicious revenge on the part of a woman who had always bowed to his oppressive authority? I don't know whether you can understand, Mr. Burns....'

'Oh, I understand very well, madam. I'm not the cold detective, the thinking machine, that you might imagine. I do have sentiments.'

'I know, Mr. Burns,' said the young woman, placing her hand on his arm. 'I notice that.'

'I do have a certain experience with women,' continued Daren, rubbing his head, 'but I admit to being surprised when she kissed me after such a stinging slap. I fully understood that there was more to it than a sudden passionate revelation. But we saw each other again, and I realised that Alice was more than just a beautiful object.'

'And I,' said Alice, with a tender smile at her companion, 'realised that the rascal I was seeing, just to spite Andrew, wasn't so much of a rascal after all. But I can understand your surprise, Mr. Burns.'

'But no!' replied Owen gaily. 'That's what makes the world go round.' Then, turning to Daren: 'By the way, Mr. Bellamy, I've been thinking about you lately. About the Miller case.'

'What, that old business?'

'Rest assured, I'm not talking about re-opening the dossier. I'd just like to share my thoughts with you from an intellectual point of view. How to put it... to show you I'm not as mediocre a detective as I appeared the last time, at Raven Lodge. No, don't contradict me. Some of your witticisms at my expense gave away your thoughts. Your alibi for Mrs. Miller's murder seemed iron-clad, but it wasn't. And I could easily have shown that, had I been in charge of the investigation.'

A feline look appeared in Bellamy's eyes.

'You surprise me, Mr. Burns.'

'In fact, after an analysis of the facts, I realised that the crucial time—between half-past nine and half-past ten corresponded to the time you were at the piano singing your heart out. The piano—I checked this—was in a corner of the room and you were showing your back dressed as a cowboy in hat and scarf. And who resembles a cowboy more than another cowboy?'

'I see... An accomplice looking like me took my place during that hour, wearing identical clothes to mine. And what about the voice?'

'Well, you weren't talking, you were singing. As the professionals know well, singing has the particular virtue of making accents disappear. Obviously, not just anyone could have done it, only someone reasonably accomplished. Then I remembered you'd met a lot of people during the period you were playing the piano in bars.'

Daren shook his head and laughed:

'All right, Mr. Burns. From a practical point of view it might just have worked. But there were about fifty people there.'

'Exactly. In the ambient brouhaha, I tend to think that the quantity of witnesses tends to diminish their quality.'

'Very well, you've made your point. But you must admit it's only speculation on your part.'

'Agreed, but I looked into it thoroughly. Now a word about the circumstances of the murder itself. According to the testimony of a young neighbour looking out of his window, as Mrs. Miller returned empty-handed after looking for her dog in the rain, she stopped dead in astonishment in front of her house. It was probably because she saw that there were lights on in the windows, which she had remembered turning off when she went out. In other words, someone had entered during her absence, and probably not someone unknown to her because the police found no evidence of a break-in. The visitor no doubt expected to find her at home, not knowing that she had gone out to find her dog. If it was her killer—in our hypothesis, you—you must have been furious to have found her absent, having expended such effort to create an alibi. You made a cursory search of the premises, and left without thinking to turn off the light, you were so upset. But then you saw her silhouette in the street.'

'Very well, Mr. Burns, things might have happened that way, but there are a dozen alternative explanations, starting with the possibility that Mrs. Miller herself had simply forgotten to turn the lights off when she went out. Don't forget that she must have been very upset that her darling dog was missing. It was the apple of her eye. And by the same token, she could have forgotten her absent-mindedness and been surprised by the lights in the windows!'

'I'll give you that point,' responded Burns with alacrity. 'But that doesn't surprise me: you have an answer for everything. I imagine, then, that you won't have any difficulty explaining the following coincidence: three weeks after the murder, the body of one Mark Keller was fished out of the Thames. He was a failed actor, who went by the name of Larry Danieli, and had been reduced to playing a music-hall clown in East End. He was about your age, with a similar physique and had been hit over the head before being thrown in the river. The date of his death corresponded to that of Mrs. Miller. The inquest at the time didn't establish any connection between the murders, which is not surprising because drowned persons don't attract much attention. On the other hand, I, knowing where to look had no trouble finding the details. So, what do you think? Nothing? For my part, I see the classic elimination of an inconvenient witness. It was much safer for you to dispose of your accomplice.'

There was an almost palpable silence, then Owen continued:

'But let's forget about all that. It's an old case. Whatever we do, we can't bring back the dead. Let's think about the present, and the future.'

'Yes, let's do that,' agreed Bellamy, his eyes like slits. 'It's much wiser.'

'A promising future for you both. Love, money, a good part of your life ahead of you. One could say you're lucky.'

'Where are you going with this, Mr. Burns?'

'Here: despite all that chance, that almost insolent chance, I'm going to give you one more. But this chance *will be your last*.'

After another stunned silence, Burns continued in a different voice:

'And, believe me, if I grant this favour, it's assuredly not because of you, Bellamy. You understand, don't you? I know everything. Everything, down to the slightest detail. From the fake nightmare of Mrs. Sanders to the trick with Cheryl's boots, not to mention the cross, and not forgetting the remarkable two-part alibi, to better establish your innocence. Real innocence, as it happens, because it wasn't you who executed the essential moves.'

After casting a glance at Alice Johnson, who was giving him an impenetrable look, Owen stood up and continued:

'I'm giving you a forty-eight-hour respite. In two days, the dogs will be let loose. You have time to think about it and decide your best course of action. Understand that I'm not in the habit of acting like this, and I don't really know why I'm doing it. No matter. Forty-eight hours, don't forget.'

24

EXPLANATIONS

July 28, 1991

André was looking at the blue porcelain elephant as usual, no doubt for the last time. And this time, he wasn't facing Dr. Moreau alone. Célia was sitting next to him on the couch, bolt upright, her fingers gripping the clip of her handbag. She was wearing a greyish-pink cotton dress that went well with her silky blonde hair. She was very tense and had every reason to be so. The day she had waited for so long had arrived.

'I thought our dossier was closed,' said the psychoanalyst, addressing André.

'It will be today.'

'That's good. Then you've followed my advice.'

'In a way. But I think we'll gain a lot of time if we put our cards on the table. You understood the last time who Célia is, I believe.'

Dr. Moreau gave the young woman an impassive look before nodding in response:

'Yes.'

'And the name of my friend Guy must have become doubly significant, because he was her brother. You were a bit late making the connection, but your question about the disused quarry made me think that it was at that moment that you had your first doubts.'

'Indeed. But even then the coincidence seemed so extraordinary that—.'

'It wasn't a coincidence.'

In the silence that followed, Moreau pursed his lips, then nodded with a forced smile.

'In that case, I believe you owe me an explanation.'

'That's why we're here. But let's start with you, Ambroise Moreau, doctor of philosophy, teaching at the University of Strasbourg in the sixties. You were simultaneously a consulting psychoanalyst. One of

147

your patients, who lived in Obernai, a town close to Strasbourg, was Mme. Jeanne Langlois—known as Janine Lamblin in another life—who became your mistress. It's useless to deny it because my wife is in possession of her mother's diary, which makes that perfectly clear.'

'I don't deny it.'

'Your relationship ended shortly before her death. You hardly knew her family, you never visited her in Obernai—which is quite understandable—and you never had occasion to visit the Messmers, obviously. On the other hand, the names of her children, whom she must have talked to you about, were familiar to you.'

Dr. Moreau nodded again and turned to Célia:

'I had occasion to meet your father, madam. Once or twice, in private. I explained to him the gravity of your mother's condition.'

'But not the rest of it?' retorted Célia sharply.

'Of course not,' he replied with a shrug of his shoulders. 'That would have been embarrassing... for everybody.'

'Very well,' continued André. 'So much for the background. And one can understand now your sudden turnaround when you advised me to drop my research, once you realised it would implicate you yourself. Now I'm going to tell you our story, monsieur, the story of my wife and myself.

'We met in the mid-eighties. Or, rather, we met again, because we'd already known each other as children in Obernai. It was she who recognised me, in fact. Célia, who was almost twenty-five, was about eight the last time I'd seen her. I hadn't been able to attend her brother's funeral and I didn't know she'd lost her father since then. The triple loss had shattered her life. Despite that, we talked about the old days, when Guy and I systematically excluded her from all our games! Which seemed like the height of stupidity, seeing the ravishing young girl she'd become. Moreover, I found it appalling that she'd had such a tragic life. We saw each other again. I'll skip the details. We were married two years later, in 1987. The following year, and this is where it becomes interesting, my wife discovered her mother's intimate diary. It contained numerous unimportant anecdotes, such as the quarrel with her husband over the gold watch which didn't work.'

'So that wasn't a personal memory,' said Dr. Moreau curtly.

'No, not that part. But the fact that Rita wore it as a medallion, yes.

148

And I acknowledge that it came back to me thanks to your know-how. But that's a detail. There are things more astonishing and more informative than that in her notes. Darling, would you care to read a few passages?'

Célia, who had already opened her handbag, took out a mauve notebook and leafed through the pages. Keeping her head down, she swallowed and began to read:

'I'm ashamed of myself. This liaison has brought me nothing. If only I had the courage, I would tell Jean-Pierre everything. God, how I wish that everything was as it was before, that this had never happened. It's terrible, I don't know what to do. Ambroise has threatened to kill me if I leave him. And I'm sure he would do it. I want my Jean-Pierre. I don't want this cold pig of a scientist who cuts my brain open whilst he takes possession of my body.'

'That's enough, darling. I think it's clear to everyone, isn't it?'

The psychoanalyst nodded his head, whilst his fingers drummed on the armrest of his chair, then declared:

'And so you think I killed her.'

'You must admit that it's vexing to see one's mistress return to the arms of her husband after an experience less satisfying than before.'

'Even so, that's hardly enough reason to kill someone.'

'Nevertheless, that's what's written there in black and white.'

After stroking his chin thoughtfully, the scientist continued, with a vindictive gleam in his eye:

'And the rest of the story? I don't understand. Why that deceitful masquerade about a film supposedly impossible to find?'

André raised his hand in a calming gesture.

'That wasn't a masquerade. Everything I said about the film was perfectly correct. Finding it had been an obsession of mine for years. And, whatever you did in the past, I'm still indebted to you for having helped me find it. I simply used it as a means to approach you. I admit it was a bit convoluted, but you can attribute that to my profession. You can believe me or not, but all those memories you brought back for me were genuine, except for the broken watch, which was recorded in the diary, and one or two others... such as the frightened face of the woman next to me, which was pure invention.'

'And does Rita Messmer really exist?'

'Of course. I can give you her address.'

149

'That's not necessary.'

'The idea was to nudge you progressively towards the murder of your ex-mistress. To lure you with an enigmatic case from the past and engage your remarkable analytic powers; to let you play detective whilst dissecting my brain; to lead you down the path, step by step... until you realised you were investigating your own crime.'

There was another silence. Dr. Moreau continued to drum the armrest.

'I see,' he said eventually. 'As a Machiavellian exercise, I take my hat off to you. Not to mention your acting talents.'

'I was only partly acting, as I told you. But it was Célia who had tracked you down before I put the plan into place. That was why we came to live here in Orville. It was easy after that, through Mme. Christine, to approach you in a natural manner. You and Professor Jelenski, whom she had also suggested we consult.'

'Professor Jelenski,' repeated Dr. Moreau pensively. 'Perhaps you know what happened to him? He was found at the foot of his stairs yesterday, with his neck broken.'

'Yes, so we heard. It's not surprising, with such a steep staircase.'

That statement wasn't false in itself, thought André. He'd always thought that staircase was dangerous. On the other hand, he had never imagined for a moment that his wife would suddenly push the astronomer in the back to guarantee his silence, as if in a fit of madness, even though she had acted bizarrely that night. He could still hear her saying: *It could be dangerous for us if he starts crying from the rooftops that we are murderers.* For her to have acted thus for their security was plausible, even though few would have taken Jelinski's claims seriously. But for her to suspect him of being Heinrich, the brother of Rita, was more disturbing. Practically speaking, such a hypothesis was plausible. But why would Heinrich have concealed his identity and pretended to be dead to his sister? That didn't make sense. It was clear that Célia was a victim of nerves, severely tested by the overlong wait to put their plan into practice and extract her vengeance—which was equally his, because they were but one since they had matched the two seashells. To play cat and mouse, let him stew in his own juice, and drive him to confess before submitting to the authorities the written proof in the hand of the victim, that was the strategy.

But it had to be said that Moreau was holding his ground for the moment. He was maintaining his calm. If André had had his doubts about his guilt—which he had never dared to share with his wife— that was no longer the case. The man's haughty and disdainful attitude had convinced him.

'Is there anything else you wish to add?'

It was too much for Célia. She leapt up from the couch like a tigress, still holding her handbag, and flung the accusation in his face:

'Anything else? How dare you? Because of you I've lost my mother, whom you killed like the coward you are. I also lost my brother.' She pulled out the photo of him pushing her on the swing. 'He died in a car accident whilst my father was at the wheel, still suffering from the pain—he must have been thinking of my mother at that very moment. After that last stroke of fate, how could he have the force to live? I witnessed first-hand his slow, painful death. You've decimated my entire family, Dr. Ambroise Moreau. You've destroyed my life forever....'

'Calm yourself, madam,' he replied in a soothing voice. 'I didn't kill anyone. If anyone murdered your mother, it was your father.'

For Célia, the affront was so great that she remained paralyzed. Slowly, Dr. Moreau stood up, opened a drawer of his desk, retrieved a notebook and leafed through it. He jotted down a few notes on a piece of paper and handed it to me.

'These are the personal contact numbers of the officer in charge of the investigation. With a bit of luck, they're still valid. We had the opportunity to get to know each other later, as a result of another case. He gave me his impressions about Jeanne's death. I urge you to talk to him. He can explain better than I.'

André automatically pocketed the piece of paper without taking his eyes off his wife's ashen face, as she said in a voice deformed by hate:

'You killed my mother and now you accuse my father.'

'You forced me to do so, madam, admit it.'

'You forced me, too,' she screamed, just before pulling a small silver pistol out of her bag, with which she proceeded to drill three holes in Dr. Moreau's forehead.

25

LIVERPOOL

Late February, 1911

In a miserable hotel room, in the heart of the port area of Liverpool, Alice was lost in thought. Her forehead pressed against the dirty glass of the only window in the room, she watched the day extinguish the last of the street lights. The sky was grey, the bricks dark, the buildings gloomy and the air impregnated with the nauseous smell of the port. She had rarely seen such a desolate landscape in her life. But at that moment, it appeared wonderful to her.

She and Daren were at the dawn of a new life. She was certain of it. Chandra had made her understand that the moment would come soon. He knew, just as he knew what they'd done and what she was going to do, what she was going to do to *him* that night, after they'd contemplated the stars together... Wait for Andrew to fall asleep, get up and retrieve *The King in Yellow* from its hiding place—judiciously concealed amongst the logs—go to the drawing room to burn it in the hearth and be surprised by him... My God, what it had cost her to strike that man she admired so much in such a cowardly manner! But she'd had no choice. It was *written....*

Just as it was written that the considerate Owen Burns would give them a chance before he did what he had to do. A chivalrous gesture on his part. She would miss him, too. A charming man, with excellent manners, as intelligent as he was understanding. There had been electricity between them from the first. No man had ever complimented her for the gracefulness of her hands.

The same evening he issued his ultimatum, whilst Daren was pacing up and down like a caged lion, turning plans of escape over in his mind, the "truth" appeared to her. Chandra's words came to her:
You will realise its usefulness at the right time, when a new life is offered to you.... All history is written in the stars.

And theirs in particular. She'd known it when their halves of seashell had matched.

She hadn't quite understood the notion of the marvellous colour, unique and invisible, but it must have something to do with divine light... Weren't the sublime reflections from the mother-of-pearl a clear symbol?

It had been clear to her that the two halves of seashell now needed to be united, as they had been originally. So that their marvellous history could be repeated; so that a new life could be offered to her and Daren.

She'd taken the precious receptacle which Chandra had given her and used a few drops of the milky liquid on the two halves in order to unite them. Once the surplus glue had been wiped off with a wet sponge, she'd been able to admire the astonishing solidarity of the finished article. Every trace of the breakage had been erased. It was extraordinary!

Needless to say, Daren, when she'd shown him the result, had become a bit testy. In a typically masculine way, he'd talked about the urgency of planning their future in a practical manner.

'How can you think about such nonsense at a time like this? We have to make a decision this very evening! Because tomorrow we have to clear off. Hell's bells, why didn't I bump off that arrogant phony of a detective immediately? I shouldn't have listened to you.'

So saying, he'd shot a furious look at his Smith and Wesson pistol, which, he'd explained, could turn out to be a useful companion, given the numerous obstacles in their path.

Alice had pointed out the futility of such an act, given that Owen Burns would inevitably have taken precautions against such an eventuality. In fact, she hadn't been convinced of that, but the idea of the detective being yet another victim of Daren's hate was intolerable. They'd left a long enough trail of dead bodies already. And, anyway, it didn't matter much since she'd "understood."

'America, France, Scotland... it doesn't much matter which,' he'd ranted. 'But we have to make a decision. And when I think we won't even be able to lay our hands on that inheritance, through lack of time, when it could have been so useful....'

Calmly, she'd explained the usefulness of the assembly she'd created.

'What an idea, darling! You're starting to lose your mind,' he'd replied, trying to maintain his calm. 'But I do admit that I, too, feel like a rat trapped at the bottom of a well.'

The following morning, they'd taken the first train to Liverpool. Daren had remembered an old Scottish friend who owned a fisherman's hut in one of the most remote regions of the country, a hovel he only lived in during the summer, and which was therefore available now. Hiding there had been the best solution he could think of for the time being, but he'd decided to stop over in Liverpool in case he changed his mind.

During the afternoon, Alice had gone for a stroll in the port and visited the Cunard Line office. She had noticed a French traveller who inspired confidence and who had just purchased a ticket for the *Lusitania*, departing the next day. The man had been surprised by her request, but had eventually accepted, probably because of her beautiful blue eyes.

When she'd found Daren back in their room, she had proudly reported the event. Her companion—still edgy—had let out a nervous laugh:

'And you think that snail-eater is going to preciously guard that shell on your behalf?'

'He made me a promise.'

'For a purpose he knows nothing about? You can't be serious, my sweet. I bet he chucked it in the sea as soon as your back was turned.'

'I saw in his eyes that he would keep his promise.'

'He probably read a different kind of promise in your eyes.'

'Never mind, as long as he keeps his word. I *had* to do it. Chandra had made it clear to me.'

'Chandra! Always Chandra! Anyone would think you were in love with him. In fact, I could have believed it, if you hadn't....'

'Stop, please. Don't turn the knife in the wound. If I did it, it was for us... so that we could stay together always.'

'Yes, until death do us part,' replied Daren. 'Which is what's likely to happen if we waste our time on such nonsense.'

'In fact, you haven't told me yet what you plan to do. Have you made a decision?'

'Not yet. But I've narrowed it down. It's either South America or the Scottish cabin.'

After that Daren had left. When Alice saw him again that evening, she discovered that he'd decided on the latter. If they took the early morning train, they'd be in Glasgow before noon. And from there to Morar, a small village near the cabin, which they should reach just as the delay allowed by Owen was due to expire.

Alice agreed without a word. A strange smile appeared on her lips. She was thinking about a construction site she'd happened to pass during the afternoon. A handsome young workman, very sure of himself, had wanted to try his luck and had struck up a conversation with her. He'd supplied her with certain information about the construction plans.

'It's the most flexible solution, given our modest circumstances, darling,' she heard Daren say. 'If only we had a bit more in the way of funds.'

'But we do,' she replied in a calm voice.

'What?'

'I'm a very resourceful woman, you should know that by now. I didn't spend the entire afternoon mincing about with the French. A great opportunity presented itself in the Cunard Line offices, which I seized with both hands. A fire alarm terrified the cashier and the other visitors, but not me... If you see what I mean.'

'Yes, indeed!' exclaimed Daren, his eyes wide. 'How much, darling? How much?'

'It's not a huge amount, but it will help out. I didn't have time to count it, but it filled both hands, and it wasn't only one-pound notes.'

'You're marvellous, darling,' exclaimed Daren, taking her in his arms, 'but you're only telling me now.'

'Yes, only now. You upset me a little just now with your sarcastic comments about my "French" initiative. Don't try to understand women, my dear. Even with your experience, you'll never succeed completely.'

'Yes, I'll have to accept that eventually. But never mind about that. Where's the money?'

'In a safe place. I had to improvise. I was afraid I might get caught.'

It was after midnight when Daren and Alice, armed with a torchlight, reached the construction site where she'd met the young workman. After having groped around on the muddy ground spiked with metal rods, she indicated one of the deep holes which punctuated the vast rectangular space.

'It's there, darling.'

'Down there?' he asked anxiously. 'But that's more than ten feet deep. What were you thinking, throwing it down there? And how do you propose getting down?'

'With a rope. There must be one around.'

A few moments later, Daren reached the bottom of the excavation, by means of a rope attached to an iron bar embedded in the concrete.

'I can't see anything,' he grumbled. 'There's only mud and stones.'

'I'm coming,' said Alice. 'I think I know where it must have fallen.'

She appeared next to Daren, who was surprised to see his Smith and Wesson in her hand.

'It has to be this way, my darling,' she whispered, 'for us to be united forever.'

The sound of a detonation froze the expression of surprise on Daren's face forever. After which Alice attached the end of the rope to a large stone and threw it up into the open hole above her. Then, with surprising energy, she dug a recess, into which she rolled Daren's body. She lay down beside him and wrapped her arm around his neck, gun in hand, pointing to her open mouth.

With the finger on the trigger, she told herself it would indeed be strange if anyone spotted them from above, covered in mud and hidden in the recess, any more than they would be concerned about a rope attached to a stone. In a few hours, the labourers would start work. They would fill the excavations with concrete and seal forever their last embrace.

26

THE ESCAPE

July 31, 1991

The sky was overcast that afternoon, and the temperature had dropped a few degrees. Under the greyness of the clouds, the old quarry appeared more dull, more abandoned. After having inflicted a gaping wound on nature, man had abandoned his victim in utter indifference. The place was so desolate it seemed to have even frightened its exploiters and other invaders. Other than the two men standing on the edge, and a few marauding crows, there was not a living soul around. Only their respective vehicles, parked side by side, injected a technical note into a purely mineral and vegetal universe.

For André, the view in front of him matched his sullen mood perfectly. The man next to him, Charles Lambert, a retired *gendarmerie* officer, was still alert despite his seventy years. André had telephoned him the evening of Dr. Moreau's death whilst Célia was sound asleep, having taken a powerful sleeping pill. He'd been pleasantly surprised when the other had picked up the phone, and even more so when he'd agreed to meet him two days later.

André was careful not to tell Célia about his rendezvous, or that he'd previously noted down the *gendarme's* contact information. The scene two nights ago when she'd suddenly executed Ambroise Moreau was as present in his mind as the supposed suicide of Jeanne Langlois, at the spot where he was now standing. He had held his wife tightly in his arms as she had collapsed in tears after perforating the psychoanalyst's skull three times. By a stroke of luck, nobody had heard the shots, so he'd dragged the body, its mouth and eyes frozen in astonishment in death, down to the garage, where he'd placed it in the boot of the late psychoanalyst's car. Then they'd left as discreetly as possible, André having pocketed the keys to the house and the car. As far as they could recall, nobody had noticed them arrive. The fact that Ambroise Moreau lived on the edge of a forest had no doubt saved their bacon. It would very likely be several days before anyone noticed his absence. He would therefore have time to dispose of the body and return the car to the garage, after removing all traces from the boot.

There again, just as for the death of Jelenski, they'd been lucky. If they didn't make any mistakes, they'd get away with it. The biggest danger was Célia herself. She'd been delirious for a good part of the morning the day before, but seemed to have recovered afterwards, and had promised him that all was well and she would rapidly recover her forces. She even seemed happy to have eliminated by her own hand the monstrous individual who had done so much evil. From now on, she would keep a clear head. She hadn't raised any objection when he'd told her he'd be away most of the next day, on the pretext of seeing a director. She had assured him he could leave with an easy conscience.

The voice of Charles Lambert brought him out of his reverie:

'It's here, at our feet. But don't get too close, I beg of you! It's a fifty-foot drop, straight down, and it's sandstone. In other words, it would make a mess.'

'You're sure this is the spot?'

'Quite sure. I remember because of that mound behind us, which gave us food for thought.' He turned round. 'You see? It's only three feet high, but it's enough to hide behind if you're lying flat. Or hiding something, which the witnesses might not have noticed as they ran forward.'

'Where were they exactly?'

'A hundred feet or more away. The two friends, whose names I've forgotten, but who had no reason to harm Mme. Langlois, were over there near the clump of trees to the north-east. We're south here. Jean-Pierre Langlois was to the north, in open space. The two friends were taking their sandwiches out of a bag when they heard Mme. Langlois cry out. They turned round and just had time to see her go over the edge. Langlois himself was looking north, and saw the same thing as the friends when he turned round. They all rushed over and arrived at the same time. They could only watch the tragedy. It was hard to envisage murder, as you can see for yourself. And suicide didn't seem to fit the circumstances. So all that was left was accidental death, which is what was accepted.'

160

'Accepted by you or by the inquest?' asked André, giving his companion an enquiring look.

'By the inquest,' replied Charles Lambert, his eyes narrowing. 'For my part, I had my suspicions of the husband. To say the least. He was an important man who didn't look down on you, whom I'd met once or twice. Nevertheless, in these kinds of cases, where there are conjugal problems, nine times out of ten it's the surviving spouse who's responsible. And I sensed it as well. I read it in his eyes, even though they were red with grief. Deep down, he must have sincerely regretted the loss of his wife. But that's often the case: it's preferable to eliminate an annoying wife than to repudiate her. Don't ask me why. Then there was his mistress, a beautiful German, the Bavarian type, as I recall. I questioned her a few days later, because she wasn't there when it happened. With her, it was even more obvious, I could read all the horror of the murder in her big blue eyes. Even if she wasn't an accomplice, she knew her lover had done the deed. Except I couldn't prove anything. Physically, it was hard to see it as murder.'

'And the witnesses hadn't seen anything suspect or strange?'

'Alas, no. Except that the two friends mentioned birds.'

'What do you mean?'

'Birds wheeling around above the victim. But they weren't sure. It was just an impression.'

'Maybe crows like those?' asked André, looking up at the sky.

'Maybe, but what of it? The sole possibility, in my opinion, is that Langlois had hidden some kind of trap behind the mound. Something like a jack-in-the-box, with who-knows-what kind of diabolical mechanism to frighten his wife. But it's difficult to argue because the couple didn't see anything of the sort. And I did ask them about it... Ah, foul creature,' shouted Lambert suddenly, as a crow skimmed his hat, cawing loudly.

André watched the bird disappear in a flurry of wings. He frowned and stood there for a while before snapping his fingers:

'Suppose they were bats?'

'Bats?' repeated the old *gendarme* in surprise.

'Yes, the birds seen by the witnesses.'

'In bright daylight?'

'Why not? They could have been chased from a cave.'

'You've got an idea in the back of your mind, my lad.'

161

'Yes. Jeanne Langlois drowned her sorrows in alcohol. I've just remembered that in her delirium she saw bats everywhere.'

'That rings a bell, but what's the relevance?'

'You or that bird jogged my memory. With my friend Guy—the Langlois's son—we tried to make a boomerang, and were given an earful by his father. So I was astonished when, later, I saw him practising by himself in the forest. With a much bigger model, painted black. That's what I just remembered.'

'Black like a bat!' exclaimed Lambert, punching his fist in his hand. 'He must have launched a couple whilst the two friends weren't paying attention, and in such a way they flew past the victim, who was frightened and lost her balance.'

After a pregnant silence, during which André thought bitterly about Célia's misplaced vengeance, Charles Lambert continued:

'What do you plan to do? I don't suppose you want to tell your wife about it.'

'No. I'm afraid she wouldn't be able to stand the shock. And you?'

'After so many years, what could I do? And Langlois has largely paid his debt. It's awful what happened afterwards. To lose his son like that....'

He sighed and added:

'If you have the time, I'll buy you a beer.'

'Good idea. But only if you promise not to make me breathe into a balloon afterwards.'

***

On the way back André couldn't stop thinking about Dr. Moreau, who'd been right about everything. Not just the guilt of Célia's father, but his advice not to rake up the ashes of the past. In the final analysis, Célia and he had tricked themselves. Their convoluted plan had turned against them. Not only had they punished an innocent man, but they were now in deep trouble themselves. As much from a legal point of view as a mental one. Whatever happened, it would leave a scar on their psyches. Would their marriage survive? He would do everything in his power to save it. He had to protect Célia, that was all that mattered from now on. And in the immediate, he had to dispose of Moreau's body, which was easier said than done.

He was back home by nine o'clock that evening. How would he manage not to give anything away to Célia? That was what he was asking himself as he opened the door. Immediately, he sensed that something was wrong. There were too many lights on, too many clothes scattered about, too many bags and suitcases....

When Célia appeared, he was shocked. She smiled at him strangely. She had coloured spots and streaks on her face... Blood, he realised fearfully. Had she slashed her veins? No, they were intact.

'Good evening, darling,' she said in an unrecognisable voice. 'I'm glad you're back... If you only knew... But we have to hurry!'

'Why?'

'We have to leave quickly. I think it's too late to rectify the situation by now.'

'What situation?'

'I've killed Christine. I saw she'd just got back. Why are you looking at me like that? Don't you understand? She was none other than Rita! Didn't you notice that she was away each time you went to Brittany? It was obvious, wasn't it? Her so-called feeble voice and all the rest.' She gave a sinister laugh. 'They thought they would trick us, the two of them, she and her brother Heinrich disguised as an astrologer. The two of them, did I say? The three of them. Moreau was in on the plot as well. But they made a big mistake: they underestimated me!'

'Tell me I'm dreaming. You haven't killed Christine, have you?'

'Yes, of course. And I took great care. I thought about that Hitchcock film we saw the other night, with Anthony what's-his-name.'

'Psycho.'

'Yes, that's it. The shower scene. But I really think I did it better. It's too bad we haven't the time to go back there. You would be proud of your Cassilda, darling. Don't stand there with your arms dangling, we have to leave.'

'Where?'

'To Carcosa. Where else? Use your brain!'

Two hours later, at the wheel of Dr. Moreau's car, and with his body still in the boot, André was driving at breakneck speed. Célia, who was smiling at him from the passenger seat, had lost her mind, temporarily he hoped. After seeing the butchery in Christine's kitchen, he'd convinced himself that there was so much madness in the scene that no one would dream of looking for the assailant amongst her peaceful neighbours. Only an itinerant madman could have been responsible. They still had a slight chance to get away with it. (Cleaning up Christine's kitchen was unthinkable.) The only link which could point to them was Dr. Moreau, because André was known to have visited him frequently. Hence, getting rid of the body was now their top priority. And arranging a couple of details in their own house to make their departure appear voluntarily.

Without quite knowing why, he'd taken the western direction, towards Brittany. Was it because he'd seen the King in Yellow there the last time? And couldn't he see him now, in the glare of his headlights? With his yellow rags, and turned towards him to show the large gold watch he was wearing as a medallion. André gritted his teeth and shook his head. No! It was a hallucination. Célia was trying to transmit her madness to him. But it wouldn't work, he knew how to resist.

Like Ulysses blocking his ears, so as not to hear the call of the sirens, André tried not to listen to the strange song his wife was intonating. No doubt the famous "Cassilda's song". He'd described it in too much detail not to recognise it. When she stopped, it was to claim, with her hand raised theatrically:

'Beware, Carcosa, Alice is coming!'

'Why "Alice,"?' asked André after a while. 'There's no Alice in my play, as far as I know.'

'Because of *Alice in Wonderland*. Have you forgotten your classics?'

Despite the freshness of the night, the atmosphere was heavy and oppressive inside the vehicle. The tension, which had risen several notches over the last few hours, was certainly a factor.

'Carcosa, wonderland?' he retorted, his brow moist. 'Don't make me laugh. It's more likely the land of nightmares.'

Célia seemed not to have heard. Her eyes wide, she looked without seeing at the road being voraciously swallowed by the car. After a while, she said:

'We'll soon be going through the mirror. Why am I Alice, my darling? Because Alice, A-L-I-C-E is an anagram of Célia. Have you never noticed?'

'And for me, did you find something?'

'For André? Of course. There's Daren D-A-R-E-N. It's Nordic and not so common, I agree, but it works. There again, I suppose, being an intellectual, you never thought about it.'

Looking at her out of the corner of his eye, he noticed she was now playing with a fob watch.

'Where did you find that, darling?'

'But it's Camilla's, of course. The one that doesn't work any more.'

'Do you mean Rita's?'

'Yes, the one she gave you the other day.'

André sighed and concentrated on his driving, for he noticed that the road ahead was going into a long curve along a sort of corniche. He sensed the perspiration running down his forehead. He needed to be doubly careful. But, due to staring fixedly at an undulating road, his fevered mind superimposed his own thoughts... A strange procession of images... First, *The King in Yellow*, the book and then its eponymous hero, followed by other personalities which he'd revived in his play... Then the white staircase, the old woman in the rain, the railings, the silhouette of the killer, the gold watch on the wet pavement... From the boot, Dr. Moreau seemed to whisper in his ear:

'*... not just the souvenir of a film... but of a personal and disquieting souvenir buried in the very depths of your memory.*'

André asked himself if, there too, the psychoanalyst hadn't been right.

'Ah, no,' cried Célia gaily. 'I was wrong. It's working again.'

'What are you talking about?'

'The watch.'

'Don't be silly. It's never worked.'

'I can assure you... Oh, but it's incredible, *the hands are going backwards*. Look darling.'

Intrigued despite himself, André leaned across....

As he sensed that the wheels were no longer following the movements of the steering wheel, he realised his error in horror. And, as if to bring him supplementary proof, an infernal noise of crumpled metal followed....

27

AN ALMOST PERFECT PLAN

A horrible grinding of metal... a frightful shock, as if a meteorite had crashed... Then hammerings worthy of the forges of Hell... Sounds of glass breaking, of screeching metal... The floor jolting, as if under pressure from a seismic shock, before rolling on its side and ending up in place on the roof....

Then the night suddenly following the day, and silence following the infernal din... The sky opened its faucets and a torrential rain came down... A shadow fell on the pavement... What the devil was that woman doing out on a night like this?... She should have been at home, in the warmth, waiting for him... He'd told her he'd probably drop by that evening... But no, she wasn't home... That's why he'd left her house in a rage... He wanted to kill her, but she wasn't there! But it was only a temporary setback... There, there she is, she's stopped... She seems to have lost something... It's the moment... Now she's running away... "You can run, my little Jane, but it won't change anything, your hour has come"... Knowing the area well, he'd taken a passageway to take her from the rear... There, a pile of bricks... The fatal weapon.

"If she thinks I'll take pity on her because of those goggle eyes, she's mistaken." And he raised his hand holding the brick and struck her hard... Then a second time... And again, until her blood mixed with the rain streaming on the paving stones.

But suddenly she gets up... She advances inexorably towards him, unaffected by the violent blows he rains on her. Her face is as white as the hands reaching for him... "No, it's not possible"... He utters a scream which pierces his own eardrums....

Daren Bellamy woke up suddenly, his brow moist and his heart beating fast... What a horrible nightmare, he thought, whilst his eyes adapted to the light... It wasn't the first time, but this time he'd lived it with a rare intensity... He was still feeling the sticky contact of the blood on his hands... Worse still, he felt multiple spots of pain all over his body, as if Jane's ghostly avenger had beaten him up... But where the devil was he? There were inert bodies in front of him and to his side... And everywhere you could hear moans and plaintive cries.

Only now did he realise that one nightmare was hiding another, far more real. The train had just derailed... He couldn't have told under what circumstances, because he'd been asleep, but it had visibly ended badly. There didn't seem to be any survivors around him. He himself only seemed to have suffered superficial wounds, except for that oozing gash on his wrist. He'd been lucky, once again....

He managed to get out of his compartment and explored the nearby ones. It was enough to make one sick. Some bodies inert, others moving feebly, horrible moaning noises... Those escaping unscathed were relatively rare.... Amongst them was a pretty blonde woman, blocked by two bodies, calling out "thief". When their looks crossed, she indicated the window.

Outside, he saw a figure legging it towards some trees, a handbag in his hand. In the blink of an eye, Daren took in the situation. An odious vulture had profited from the occasion by stealing her belongings. Daren was not a charity-worker, but in certain situations he knew how to make himself one. He jumped out of the train and set off in hot pursuit of the fugitive.

Five minutes later, he found the pretty blonde amongst the escapees forming a group outside the train.

'I wasn't able to catch your thief, but I think he dropped his loot. This is yours, I believe,' he said, holding out a pretty suede travel bag.

A pair of beautiful blue eyes filled with gratitude looked up at him.

'Thank you, sir. Thank you very much.'

'I don't think he had time to take your money, madam. The bag was still closed when I found it in the grass.'

'Oh, it's not a question of money. Just personal effects, to which I'm very attached. Really, I don't know how to thank you.'

'Just tell me your name and I'll be happy.'

'Alice,' said the young woman with a smile. 'Alice Johnson.'

In fact, Daren didn't stop there. He made it clear he'd like to see her again and talk to her in more agreeable circumstances.

A week later, they had dinner together at *The Founders Arms*, a charming restaurant overlooking the Thames. Judging by the smiles they exchanged, the tragic railway accident seemed like a distant memory.

'Did you remember to bring what I asked?' said Daren, as coffee was being served.

'Yes,' said Alice, with an embarrassed smile. 'But it must seem odd to you that a simple seashell could be so precious.'

'Your grandmother's good luck charm, as I recall?'

'Yes, she made me promise, on her deathbed, that I would keep it in memory of her. And I thought of it instinctively, even in the midst of that awful tragedy.'

'And I ran after a thug, despite all the wounded lying around. We're dominated by our reflexes in such moments. And here we are, not knowing a thing about each other.'

Noticing her companion stealing a glance at her wedding ring, she said solemnly:

'I suppose you realise I'm married?'

'How could it be otherwise for such a beautiful woman? But you haven't told me about your husband. What does he do?'

Alice had only just begun her description when Daren interrupted her:

'Johnson. Andrew Johnson. That name rings a bell. Don't tell me he works for the Sanders company?'

'But yes! Why do you ask?'

'Mrs. Victoria Sanders' maiden name is Bellamy.'

'Why, yes. Are you related?'

'She's my sister.'

'What a small world,' observed Alice, astonished by the coincidence, but not sure whether to rejoice or not.

For each had sensed a strong reciprocal attraction, although more subconscious for Alice. As for Daren, he felt already that it would not be one of those passing relationships he was used to. Instinctively, he suppressed his usual direct approach.

As soon as Alice had placed her precious half-shell on the table, Daren declared, putting his hand into an inside pocket:

'I didn't want to talk about it last time, for fear of appearing opportunist. Believe it or not, I also inherited a piece of seashell from my mother. I don't know the accompanying history, except that it meant a lot to her. I thought it might interest you.'

169

After he had pulled the partial shell out of a velvet bag and placed it on the table, Alice exclaimed:

'But they're very similar! What a coincidence. No, you're pulling my leg, Daren,' she added with a laugh. 'I'm not that naive.'

'I was afraid you would think that, but thank you for the "Daren," anyway.'

'How did you manage to find such a close match?' said Alice, automatically connecting the two pieces. She looked up suddenly:

'But they're a perfect fit,' she stammered.

'Now who's pulling whose leg?'

'But it's true! See for yourself.'

Daren was stunned by the extraordinary coincidence. From that moment on, there was no stopping their growing passion for each other. But Alice could not accept the idea of separating from her husband. Not because she loved him—she hadn't for some time, and even suspected him of having an affair with his new secretary—but out of principle and her financial situation. As she explained:

'If I leave Andrew, I shall be penniless, and I can't resign myself to a Bohemian life.'

'Neither can I, but listen. I'm not rich now, but my sister is. And I have a plan for changing that.'

Over the next few days, they went over the details of Daren's plan. Alice was now convinced that it was Fate that had thrown them together, that it had been written in the stars, and that the challenges they would have to face, tragic though they may be, were also written there. The elimination of Victoria was just part of a grander scheme. She was prepared to follow Daren, even to Hell.

Daren had made it clear to her that his position as sole legatee would automatically make him the prime suspect, so he had to have an iron-clad alibi. It was she, therefore, who would have to carry out the menial chores. On top of that, it was vital that their affair remained secret and even unthinkable. To pull the wool over everyone's eyes, he would pretend to make a vulgar pass at her, which she would rebuff in disgust. At the same time, she would pretend to be jealous of her husband's secretary and would feign a few domestic rows. The weekend in the country would be the perfect occasion to put their plan into execution, since the forecast promised heavy snow. Daren, who had recently read *The King in Yellow*, proposed using the legend of that cursed book, reputed to drive its readers to murder or suicide. All that was needed was to place a copy on his sister's bedside table. Alice would draw attention to herself and arrange to leaf through it—her and no one else—and proclaim that there were only verses out of a play and there was no author's name on the cover. Alice herself would also need an alibi, even if not as solid as Daren's, for two separate times, in order to trick the investigators.

During the fatal night, at around four o'clock in the morning, she would set her watch back two hours and cry out in order to waken her husband. Beforehand, she would have arranged a meeting with Victoria on the ground floor—in the drawing room, for example—on the pretext of a grave personal matter concerning her brother, the only subject which could have enticed her to meet in the small hours. Failing that, she would strike her a mortal blow whilst she was asleep.

After having played the role of the worried woman, and preceding her husband in the unlikely case that he would find the willpower to get out of bed, she would leave their bedroom. She would deliver the fatal blow to Victoria, drag her body into the woodshed, and return to her room. She would explain to Andrew that his boss had got up as a result of a terrible nightmare, and would manoeuvre him into getting her a glass of hot milk, so that the investigators would later suspect him of administering a sleeping draught at that time, supposedly half-past two in the morning. In his position as deputy director, ambitious to take over, he would make a good suspect. After he'd gone back to sleep, Alice would put her watch forward to the correct time. And, later that morning, the lifeless body of Mrs. Sanders would be discovered, seemingly having had an unfortunate fall, as a result of her nightmare. Daren would return from London at about that time, blessed with a solid alibi.

Such was their base plan. But Daren, whose twisted mind had been further influenced by reading hundreds of detective novels, planned to enhance their strategy if the snowfall was favourable. As soon as he learnt that Cheryl, who had been detained in London, intended to take the first train in the morning, he saw how he could take advantage of that fact. Cheryl Chapman would become their unwitting accomplice. He would feign attraction for her, with the aim of further drawing attention away from his affair with Alice.

'And if all goes well, darling,' he explained to her shortly before the fatal day, 'if everything is covered in virgin snow, we can put our optional plan into effect. In that case, in addition to providing our alibis, the immaculate whiteness of the snow will make murder seem to be a physical impossibility. Victoria will be found in the middle of a snow-covered field, having apparently hit her head on a stone, having left only her own footprints behind her.'

'But how is that possible?' asked Alice, looking dreamily at her lover.

'I'll explain to you, my darling. And I confess I'm rather proud of myself. It's a little complicated, certainly, but....'

'Kiss me first. Women need tenderness in order to be attentive.'

EPILOGUE

I didn't see Owen Burns again until the end of April. Whenever I came to London seeking news of him, he was away. Amongst other trips, he'd travelled to Paris to solve the riddle of the leopard-man, a dangerous robber who had foiled the Sûreté there. The press had heaped praise on his contribution, no doubt with the objective of stigmatising the French police even more. On the other hand, very little had been written about the Sanders affair, other than the disappearance of Alice Johnson and Daren Bellamy two months earlier. No news since then. Given Owen's strange remarks on the subject, I didn't feel like asking Inspector Wedekind. I nevertheless thought that their double disappearance was most suspicious.

He greeted me warmly when I eventually tracked him down and divulged the identity of the culprits and their diabolical plan.

'It's incredible,' I declared. 'People don't disappear like that. Have you any idea where they might be?'

'None,' replied Owen, shaking his head. 'In any case, I doubt that they've left this island of ours. The passenger lists of all the maritime companies have been examined, to no avail. I don't know, Achilles, I really don't know.'

'But why did you warn them? Their crimes were not such as to invite clemency.'

'I don't know,' he replied, with a thoughtful finger on his chin. 'But did you fully understand what I explained to you?'

'Of course. Whom do you take me for? They wanted to inherit Victoria Sanders' wealth, they pretended to detest each other to throw everyone off the track, the trick of the book, the delayed alibi of Daren and of Alice, who put her watch back to trick her husband, and the rest of it.'

'Yes, it was very well played. Admit that you never suspected any of it.'

'True. The beautiful Alice played us all for fools. As much in the role of jealous wife as that of disgusted wife. And the bad dream she'd had in her room, about a door knob turning, so as to induce us to swallow the tale of Mrs. Sanders' nightmare.'

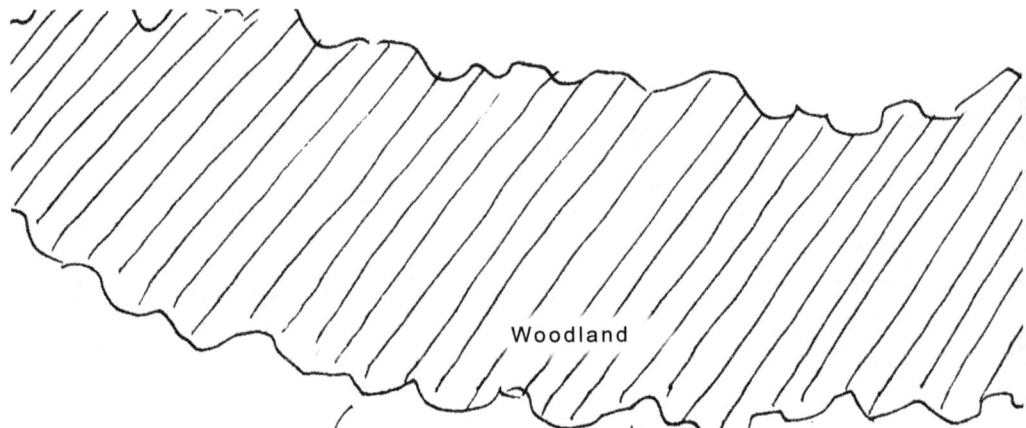

Woodland

First trip of Daren and
Cheryl, followed by
Alice and her dog

→ Footprints of Alice
wearing Cheryl's
boots (both ways)

▽ Footprints of Alice
wearing Mrs.Sanders'
ankle-boots

➡ Footprints of Daren
carrying corpse of Mrs.
Sanders

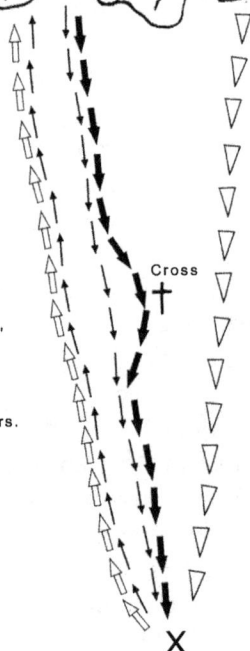

⇨ Footprints of Daren
carrying Alice on his
back

Cross

Y Fake corpse

X

Corpse of Mrs. Sanders

'I think that was Daren's idea,' observed Owen. 'No doubt copied from his favourite reading, detective novels, because it's a classic suspense scene. Who knows? He could have made a good author, if he'd put his Machiavellian mind to the theory, rather than the practice. Nevertheless, you must admit that his accomplice acted her role very well, pretending not to know whether she had dreamt or not, then invoking, without insisting, the tragic memory of the railway accident, only too real that...'

'Finally, Owen,' I cut in, 'there's the murder of Victoria Sanders in the snow. I'm not leaving until you've explained that piece of abracadabra.'

'In that case...,' said Owen, smiling. 'In fact, it's not all that complicated, given the events at our disposal, and once I was sure of the complicity of the lovers. I'll start with the meeting of Daren and Cheryl in the train which, despite appearances, was not in the least accidental. Then there was the clue of the shoes... Do you remember that Daren and Cheryl removed theirs on arrival at Raven Lodge? It wasn't by chance, either. Daren provoked the situation by deliberately omitting to wipe his snow-covered boots, thus leaving visible wet traces in the hallway, much to the annoyance of Chandra. He gave them slippers and bade them enter. That's when Alice enters the scene....

'It's five minutes past eight. She takes Cheryl's boots and goes to the woodland area using what I shall call the "passage", the few yards which separate the front of the building from the woods. It's the same "passage" she will take later to walk her dog, so as to obliterate any traces left on the snow. And it's probably where she dragged the corpse of Mrs. Sanders by its legs to hide it just after she killed her. Unless she left it in the woodshed and Daren took care of it after that? I lean towards the first solution. That young woman is stronger than she appears and Mrs. Sanders is about her weight. Be that as it may, the body was in the woods when they began their manoeuvre. But before that, Alice goes to point X—which is what we'll call the spot where the police found the body—and back. Which takes her about ten minutes. "Miss Cheryl"'s footprints are now in place. I may add that Alice was careful not to go within ten yards of the cross on her outward journey. I'll explain why this was necessary later. It's a quarter past eight. She puts Cheryl's boots back in their place, then hastens to join her accomplice, who's waiting by the body. He has removed Mrs. Sanders' ankle-boots. She puts them on and returns to Point X, using a slightly different route which we saw and assumed were the victim's last steps. At that point, we have those prints, plus Cheryl's going there and back. Are you still with me?'

'Perfectly. All that's needed now is Daren's steps going there and back.'

'Exactly. Daren, having hoisted the corpse on his back, goes out in turn to Point X, where his accomplice is waiting. He puts the body down. Alice takes off the ankle-boots and puts them on their owner's feet. They scuff the snow a little to cover their manoeuvre, Alice climbs astride Daren's back, and they return home, collecting Alice's own shoes on the way. And so we have Daren's return trip, which we were missing. Note that the depth of his footprints in both directions is about the same, given that each time he carried a woman of about the same weight. Which is what fooled the Scotland Yard expert and even me. Thus we wrongly ruled out the hypothesis of a murderer carrying a body.... By now, it's about half-past eight. After swapping his boots for the slippers, Daren hastens to the drawing room to have breakfast. Ten minutes later, Alice pays a lightning visit there, then goes out to walk her dog, using the aforementioned "passage". All clear so far?'

'Perfectly. A remarkable series of manoeuvres, in any case. I can understand how an expert like you was held in check.'

'No superfluous remarks, Achilles, if you wish to hear the rest of the story.'

'Actually, I'm beginning to work it out.'

'It's about time. So, Alice is in the woods with her dog. In the bag she's brought with her are a black wig and a violet coat... As you've guessed, she's about to play the role of the victim. Previously, she's tied her dog to a tree. If he barks, it's normal. Dogs bark whether they're being walked or not. With her blonde hair tucked under a hairnet and the black wig on her head, and perhaps a spot of make-up to resemble Mrs. Sanders, she walks, not to Point X, but to Point Y, the spot where Daren and Cheryl will make their macabre discovery later, on their own walk. The distance of Point Y from the woods is about three hundred yards, as it is for Point X. But they are separated by about one hundred yards, Point Y being much farther west. Alice, lying on the snow like a dead woman, in the same posture as the unfortunate Mrs. Sanders, awaits the arrival of the walkers.

'Daren, in the company of the ex-model, goes into the woods on the pretence of looking for the route to the cross, but in reality to scuffle the earlier footprints and to disorient his companion, for it is vital that she not remember the exact route they will take. But it's the trick with the cross which will be the key factor. Remember her testimony on the subject? She didn't actually see it, she more or less guessed where it was because her companion—who was behind her and to the side— had apparently had an unfortunate collision. It wasn't the fog which prevented her from seeing it. It was the fact that it wasn't there! It was actually a hundred yards away to the east. I'll spare you the rest of the details. Daren cleverly directed the discovery of the fake corpse. Cheryl was much too terrified to detect the trickery. They returned to Raven Lodge without further ado.

'Shortly thereafter, Alice got up and walked over their tracks, blurring them as much as possible. She then released her dog and took it for a walk over the same tracks, letting it run everywhere, further blurring the footprints. When she judged he had done enough, she went back to the house, ready to play her role as a woman devastated by the terrible news. There's nothing more for her to do, so she can take a well-earned break. The trap has been set. Cheryl will obediently follow Daren when he leads the police past the cross—a veritable beacon of the path to the body of the real Mrs. Sanders, where a whole series of footprints confirming the story converge.

'As for the traces left by Alice and her dog, too far from the scene of the crime to have played any part, they were submitted to only a cursory examination. The most that one could assume is that another person had happened to walk there. Even I hadn't thought it necessary to investigate further.'

'In that case, who else could possibly have detected evil, I ask myself?'

Curiously, Owen ignored my persiflage. With a distant look in his eye, he concluded:

'And now I think everything has been said on the matter.'

'On the matter of the footprints, yes. You've demonstrated your usual brilliance for that kind of mystery. But for the rest...no.'

'What "rest"? Haven't I been sufficiently clear about the details?'

'I'm talking about your strange indulgence for the demon lovers. Your previous evasive response wasn't good enough, as you very well know.'

There was a long silence.

'But I think I know,' I continued. 'It's because of her, isn't it? You fell for the beautiful Alice. I knew from the start. That compliment about the hands was a thinly-veiled compliment for everything about her. Or else you had a professional admiration for her, seeing as how she led you a merry dance?'

Owen was slow to respond:

'It's possible, Achilles. Quite honestly, I don't know. I even think she's no longer of this earth.'

'Why is that?'

'Because there's been no sign from her. She would have found a way to send me a thank-you message. But why all these questions? Why did I do this or that? Why does the wind blow? Why does the sun shine? Why does the earth turn? I don't have the answers, Achilles. Ask the question of the stars, I've been reliably informed that they do.'

CPSIA information can be obtained
at www.ICGtesting.com
Printed in the USA
LVHW041751110919
630729LV00012B/903/P